GHOSTS OF JAMES BAY

GHOSTS OF JAMES BAY

John Wilson

An imprint of
Beach Holme Publishing
Vancouver

This book is published by Beach Holme Publishing, 226–2040 West 12th Avenue, Vancouver, B.C. V6J 2G2. *www.beachholme.bc.ca*. This is a Sandcastle Book.

The publisher gratefully acknowledges the financial support of the Canada Council for the Arts and of the British Columbia Arts Council. The publisher also acknowledges the financial assistance received from the Government of Canada through the Book Publishing Industry Development Program (BPIDP) for its publishing activities.

The Canada Council | Le Conseil des Arts
for the Arts | du Canada

BRITISH
COLUMBIA
ARTS COUNCIL
Supported by the Province of British Columbia

Editor: Michael Carroll
Production and Design: Jen Hamilton
Cover Art: Doug Sandland
Author Photograph: Tom Shardlow

Printed and bound in Canada by Kromar Printing

National Library of Canada Cataloguing in Publication Data

Wilson, John (John Alexander), 1951-
    Ghosts of James Bay

"A Sandcastle book."
ISBN 0-88878-426-0

1. Ghosts—James Bay Region—Juvenile fiction. I. Title.
PS8595.I5834G56 2001   jC813'.54 C2001-911076-6
PZ7.W566Gh 2001

For Sue and Allan

ONE

The surface of James Bay in Northern Ontario was cold and calm the morning I disappeared. As the canoe glided along, the glassy water hardly made a sound against its hull. The rocky, tree-lined shore was only a few hundred metres away, but I could barely see it through the shroud of mist rising around me. From a hidden lake over the trees, a solitary loon cried mournfully as it patrolled its territory. The dawn sun, which had lured me out onto the water, was now only a pale disk in the bank of thicker fog rolling toward me.

That fog should have been my warning. I knew the dangers. It was September, Labour Day weekend, and the weather could change quickly and dramatically. A wind could rise from nowhere, creating choppy waves that would swamp the canoe or force me onto the shore. Fog could roll in and make me lose all sense of direction. I might paddle aimlessly for hours as the cold ate at me and hypothermia drew me into its shivering clutches. As soon as I saw the fog, I should have turned back to the camp where my father would be waking

1

up, building a fire, and cooking breakfast.

My name is Al Lister, and this was my dad's and my last day in camp and my final chance to go out in the canoe. I love canoeing. When I'm out in the wilderness with Dad, I go off in the canoe at every opportunity. On some remote lake I can lose myself in the water, the air, and the coastline drifting by. Sometimes I feel this is what it must have been like hundreds of years ago. I can almost imagine a crew of voyageurs with a load of furs paddling in front of me, or a wildly painted Iroquois raiding party slipping through the trees at my back. Of course, now the voyageurs have powerboats and the Iroquois have all-terrain vehicles, but it's nice to dream occasionally and the past offers lots of unthreatening possibilities. Then there's my father.

My dad is strange. It isn't that I don't love him or that he doesn't love me; it's just that he's sometimes a difficult person to live with. At times it's as if he comes from a different planet. Dad is so intense that I sometimes need to get away on my own, and the canoe is ideal for that. And I'm not the only person who needs to escape from Dad occasionally. Mom found him so odd that she eventually had to move us both out last year.

That was tough, having two homes, but it wasn't unusual among my buddies, and I probably ended up seeing more of both my parents when they started living apart. Maybe they both felt so guilty about the effect their split would have on me that they went overboard whenever it was their turn to see me. They were always taking me out to eat or renting a movie so we could have time together. It got so I couldn't even look at a burger, and I could have written one of those fat books that give a star rating to every movie ever made.

Anyway, one of the weirdest things Dad ever did happened when he and Mom were still together. Mom had just invited a few friends around. They were talking after dinner, and Dad was silently dreaming.

We were in the loft of our A-frame house, which is where we ate when company came because the best views over the Ottawa Valley were from there. Beside us there was a railing and a five-metre drop to the living area. I was half listening to Mom and her friends discuss the latest movies and books when Dad got up, went over to the railing, and peered into the living room. No one paid much attention; we all knew Dad. The first thing I noticed was the conversation dying around me and people looking over at the railing. I turned just in time to see Dad step over the railing and begin climbing down the wall. He had the funny, almost apologetic half smile on his face that he wore when he was doing something even he realized was a little bizarre. We all moved to the railing to see what was going on.

Dad is a rock climber. On hikes or walks he's always going off and scaling rock outcrops. For him it's an intellectual exercise—can he think his way up the challenge presented by a cliff? Dad has taught me and I've become pretty good, but I don't have his fanaticism, and I've never attempted a descent of the north face of our living room.

By the time we looked over, Dad was a third of the way down. He was holding on to the base of the railing and had his left foot on some moulding that ran across the wall. I could see his route. He had to get his right foot over and down onto the edge of the brick facing around the fireplace, then it would be easy. The only problem was that it was a long, awkward stretch. To do it he would have to reach first with his right hand and grasp the peg that protruded from the wall at shoulder level about a metre away. The peg had supported a large metal abstract sculpture, which had been taken down because Mom was planning on redecorating the room. It was the only possible handhold on the otherwise smooth wall.

Silently we watched as Dad reached out and grabbed the peg. At full stretch he tested it for strength. It seemed okay; the sculpture was a heavy one. Slowly Dad transferred his weight and stretched down for the foothold. At exactly the point where he had to commit the bulk of his weight to the peg and had no chance of recovering his hold on the railing, the peg came out of the wall. I guess he was heavier than the sculpture. In any case, for a fraction of a second Dad was in an impossible position, defying gravity. Then, with a slightly puzzled expression on his face, he peeled off the wall and fell to the floor.

Even up on the balcony we heard the crack as Dad's arm snapped beneath him. He had tried to turn on the way down but had only half managed it. For a moment there was silence. Then one of the guests asked, "Are you okay?"

It was a dumb question really—we all knew a bone had broken somewhere—but someone had to ask it. It was only later that I thought it should have been Mom who asked it.

Dumb question or not, as Dad rolled onto his good side, he replied with his longest sentence of the entire evening: "Yes, but I think I might have broken my arm."

We took him to the hospital where they put a cast on his arm and sent us home. Mom wasn't happy. "What on earth did you think you were doing?"

"Climbing down the wall," he said. One of Dad's annoying habits is answering a question literally. It used to drive Mom crazy.

"In the middle of a dinner party," she said in a voice noticeably higher than before, "you decide, out of the blue, to climb down the living-room wall? This is not normal behaviour!"

Dad looked thoughtful for a moment. "I should have tested that peg more and not made assumptions. Assumptions can kill you. It was a good reach, though."

Mom groaned in hopeless frustration. To her it had been an insane, stupid, dangerous thing to do, and she had been proved right. To Dad it had been an interesting technical problem that had popped into his mind, and the only way to solve it was to do it. He had miscalculated, but that didn't negate the fact that the underlying exercise was worthwhile. This was the pattern with Mom and Dad for a long time before they split. Sometimes they seemed to inhabit completely different worlds, and I had to live in them both. Often it was difficult.

When I went out in the canoe that morning, I wanted to be on my own for a while and get a bit of peace and quiet before the return to the stresses of school and the city. The floatplane was due in after lunch to begin moving our supplies and Dad's discoveries back to Matagami and the road south, and I had to help pack up the camp. An hour in the canoe would help me centre myself and make the transition smoother. I didn't want to cut my last canoe trip short, so I ignored the fog. And I was glad I did. If I had turned around, life would have been simple, comfortable, and safe instead of confused, exhausting, and scary. But then I would never have met Jack and the others, or had the adventure of a lifetime.

The warrior crouched among the trees, watching. The canoe, the largest he had ever seen, sat in the bay. It was held fast by the ice, but lines of open water snaked across the view, indicating that breakup was close. The long sticks that grew from the canoe lay over at an angle. Soon, as the birds returned to the open water, the ice would melt enough for the strangers to put the white wings back on the sticks and the canoe would leave. The white wings were one of the marvels of these people that the warrior did not understand. They allowed the canoe to move through the water on the wind and meant that no one had to paddle such an unwieldy craft.

The strangers were white-skinned—*kawaaposit.* They had arrived before the last cold and dark and had stayed in camp here since then. They were not good hunters, had not chosen a good campsite, and now they did not look well. One of them had died. But they did have many marvels that the warrior wanted to trade for.

The *kawaaposit* camp was in the clearing, less than the height of a tall tree in front of the warrior. It was an odd place with a wooden hut built from square trees that the strangers had brought ashore from the canoe. It was much larger, but also much heavier, than the conical teepees of the warrior's people. Obviously these creatures could not travel anywhere without their huge canoe to carry all their possessions.

Several figures, including the old hair-faced one whom the warrior assumed was the leader, were standing about in the open. This would be the obvious time to meet them, when they could see him approach and would not be startled, yet the warrior hesitated.

It was not that he was frightened; he was a *Kenistenoag* and afraid of nothing. These were his lands. His people had lived here since time immemorial when they had been placed in the world by the Great Spider. The warrior lived in complete harmony with all the land's elements. True, life was difficult sometimes when the Manitou was offended and made the game go away or the cold hard or the snow deep, but that was the way the world was. The spirits were everywhere, in the animals, the trees, even in the very earth beneath the warrior's feet. They were as real as the other people in his band, and how well or badly your life went depended on how you treated them. Permission must be asked of the spirits before a tree was cut or an animal killed and thanks must be given for the bounty they provided. If it was not done, then the spirits would be offended and make life hard for the people.

No, the warrior was not frightened. What made him hesitate was the decision made by his band. Some of the elders felt these strangers were not of this world. Certainly observation of them did suggest they were very odd and seemed to have little or no contact with the spirits. To the warrior this was peculiar, but he felt that if they were not of this world, then they could have no impact upon it and contact with them would not anger the spirits. Others thought, however, that the spirits did not want the people to make contact, and their arguments had won. The pale strangers could be watched, but there was to be no contact.

The warrior felt uncomfortable with the decision. He saw no threat and felt sure that, if he could trade for some of the strangers' wonders, he could convince his people that trade with them would be to everyone's benefit. He had to do it. Taking a deep breath and murmuring a prayer to the spirits, the warrior stood and stepped out into the pale spring sunlight.

The first man to spot the warrior standing near the trees dropped the wood he was carrying and ran in terror as if he had glimpsed a Windigo monster. His shouting alerted the others, and soon they formed a semicircle in the clearing, watching the warrior carefully. Two of the men held hatchets and one carried the long stick the warrior had heard make a loud noise and seen kill game. The warrior spread his arms wide to show he held no weapon. The hairy-faced leader stepped forward and copied the gesture. Then he spoke in the strange, halting tongue these people used. The warrior remained silent. He made the gesture for trade. Hairy Face spoke again. Obviously they did not use even the same gestures as the *Kenistenoag*. Crouching, the warrior picked up three pebbles, two small and one large. He moved the two small ones toward the stranger and the large one before himself. Then, slowly and deliberately, as if he were teaching a young child, he exchanged them.

Hairy Face turned and spoke with his companions. Three of them came forward and handed him knives. A fourth brought a leather sack from inside the hut. Turning back, Hairy Face placed one of the knives on the ground in front of him. He also took several items from the sack and added them to the pile.

The warrior stepped forward. The knife was good. The blade was long, the edge sharp, and the handle fitted comfortably into his fist. He could skin a caribou or fight equally easily with this weapon. He put it back on the ground and turned his attention to the other things. There were a number of small round disks with tiny holes punched through their centres. The warrior could not imagine what their use was, but they would be good ornaments for the women to decorate ceremonial clothing. The last item was round and had a short handle at the bottom. It was shiny and had patterns engraved on it. The warrior picked it up and examined it. The other side was startling. It was clear like water and, like a still pool on a sunny day, it reflected the sky, the trees, and the warrior's face. Yet, unlike water, it was hard to the touch. These strangers must have magic to be able to capture water this way. What other wonders did they have in the leather bag?

The warrior picked up the items and placed them in his sack. By gestures he indicated he would return to this spot with trade goods after only one sleep. Hairy Face nodded. Then he began making eating gestures with his fingers. Was he asking the warrior to stay and eat with them? The warrior shook his head, turned, and strode into the trees. He had enough to think about already now that he had made contact.

TWO

Dad and I were up on the shores of James Bay digging for buried treasure. Not gold or jewels, but arrowheads, bones, and fragments of pottery. My dad is an archaeologist and spends most of his summers camped beside ancient villages in remote corners of Quebec and Ontario digging into piles of garbage. That's what archaeologists mostly do—look through what people threw away hundreds of years ago. My feeling is that if it was garbage two thousand years ago, it's still garbage now. After all, there's a reason people throw stuff away. But Dad doesn't think like that.

"It's one of the few windows we have into the lives of people who lived before things were written down," he often says. "At a campsite in Northern Quebec we can find copper from the Arctic, obsidian from Yellowstone Park, and shells from the New England coast. That's evidence of a continent-wide trading network in place long before Europeans ever set foot here."

Okay, I accept that, but it's still a window onto a garbage tip.

The summer of my morning canoe trip was our second

dig on this particular garbage tip, or midden, as Dad called it. I had been there with him the year before, but so had a lot of other people, mostly graduate students, and they got to do all the interesting work. I had been a general dogsbody, carting loads of dirt away and keeping the tools clean. The second summer was different. I was all there was, so I had to do everything, and I had enjoyed it. Just the thought that the next trowel full of dirt might reveal some vital clue was a thrill. Not that we had found much. In fact, my moment of glory had come the year before.

Our camp had been in the same place both years. It was on the shore of James Bay, with the tents in a semicircle facing the water. There was a work tent, a cook tent, sleeping tents, and a large tarpaulin strung between the trees under which we stored tools and equipment. In the centre was a large fire pit where we sometimes cooked or roasted marshmallows on sticks. The northern edge of the camp was marked by a huge rock—a glacial erratic Dad called it. It had been dropped there when the ice sheets melted thousands of years ago, and it was great for climbing. It was almost a cube, about five metres high, and there was only one side I hadn't managed to climb. It was the side closest to the camp. It was nearly smooth and was dominated by a tricky overhang near the top. I had a lot of bruises from arguing with that overhang.

At the end of the first year's dig the crew had only come up with the usual collection of discarded arrowheads, spear points, and fire-blackened bones. It was interesting, but Dad wanted more. He believed Europeans had been into Hudson Bay before Henry Hudson in 1610. Dad said the English were looking for a Northwest Passage to Asia, or the Strait of Anian, as they called it. This would give them a shortcut to the valuable spices away from any competition with Spain. Since England and Spain were virtually at war, any discovery an explorer made would be kept secret. My father believed there had been a discovery before 1610, but that it had never been written up in the history books.

Dad based his theory on an old document that dated from the late 1500s. It had turned up in an archive in Bristol and had probably been written by a fisherman, since it talked about the cod stocks off the Newfoundland coast. One piece of it caught Dad's attention. He had told me it so many times that I knew it by heart despite the odd wording and really original spelling:

> Onn the daye following wee mett with a rotten Shippes Boatt. In itt laye a man much gonne in Starvation and neare too Death. The crewe were so afrighted by his Sicklye appearence that they but crossed themselvese and would not renedere him aid. I tooke myselfe into the Boatt and befor he perrished the man tolde mee that he was the mate from the Barcke *Jonathan* from Plymouthe whiche had comme to grief in some Ice that was swepte moste Furioslye out of a Greate Sea to the west. He talked off the wonderes of the Landes he hadde seen, Unicorns, Men with theire faces on theire chestes, and seas filled with Mermaids who had the heads and bodyes of women and the tailes of Greate Fish. Then for want of Succour he died. Truly, there are yet manye wonderes too be discovered in this Lande.

It sounded like a sailor's story to me, and the poor man was obviously delirious. The information in it was vague and ambiguous. Dad could find no record of a ship called the *Jonathan* around that time. However, he was convinced the "Greate Sea" was Hudson Bay and the strait where the ship came to grief in the ice, Hudson Strait. Dad got some support from a map that was published in 1595, fifteen years before Hudson sailed. It showed a large bay at the end of a strait that cut into North America. To Dad, this meant Hudson Bay was known before Henry sailed into it, but his ideas were scoffed at. The most his colleagues would admit was that *possibly*, a few fishermen *might* have visited the Grand Banks before John Cabot, but saying that someone had gotten into Hudson Bay that far back was laughed at. Then, in the first summer, I fell off the big rock.

It was lunch break on the final day, and I was having one last try to defeat the overhang. I failed and landed painfully back at the bottom. As I was spitting a mouthful of dirt out, I noticed something in the ground. The rock was quite far from the midden where the main work was going on, so no one was interested in digging there. I didn't think anything of it at first—all I could see was a tiny curve of something dirty—but I had been trained by years of helping my father to look for anything unusual. I called Dad over and he dug it out. His excitement grew as he uncovered something that was obviously not just another trade trinket.

"It's a coin," he said, lifting the object and turning it in the sunlight. "Very old. Looks like it might even be gold."

That sent a thrill through me—gold—but it really didn't look like much. It was round, but so covered with dirt that I couldn't make anything out.

We dug around, down almost thirty centimetres, but found nothing else. However it got there, the coin was on its own.

One of the few things Dad knew nothing about was coins so, when we returned to town, we went to see a collector. Dad knew better than to try to clean the coin without knowing what he was doing, so it was pretty grubby and still didn't look like much.

The collector was a short, dumpy man. He was old and wore half-glasses on his nose. He talked about as much as Dad, so there were a lot of silences while he worked on the coin.

I was looking at the display cases filled with odd things like groats and farthings, Dad was lost in thought, and the collector was talking to the coin under his breath. He never managed to complete a sentence: "It must be... Where is that...? Now if only I can..." At last he let out a louder than usual exclamation: "Aha!"

Dad and I turned. The collector lifted his head and seemed startled that we were still there. He looked at us silently for a while. "Yes," he said eventually, "this is very nice." Then he lapsed back into silence.

"Good," Dad said encouragingly. "But what is it and how old is it?"

"Yes, yes," the collector continued, "it's an angel, and a very nice one, too."

He seemed about to stop talking again, so I asked, "What's an angel?"

"Oh!" He seemed surprised that I didn't know. "An angel is an old English gold coin originally worth six shillings and eight pence—one-third of a pound—but later revalued up to ten shillings. They were introduced by Edward IV in 1465 and were made until old Charles I got his head chopped off after he lost the English Civil War in the 1640s." The man said "old Charles I" as if he had been a personal friend.

"But why angel?" I asked before he got too far into the list of English kings.

"Well," he continued, holding up the coin, "look here." We both moved closer and peered where he pointed with a chubby finger. "See the picture on the obverse?" We looked closer.

"St. George and the dragon?" I ventured. The collector made a noise like the one my math teacher made when someone gave a really dumb answer.

"No, no. See the halo around the head? It's the archangel Michael spearing a dragon. Hence the name." He turned the coin over. The other side had a picture of a ship carrying a coat of arms covered in fleur-de-lys and lions. There was writing around the rim on both sides, but I couldn't make out what it said. "This is unique. I've never seen one of these before." The collector quivered with excitement. "It must be worth a fortune."

"How old?" I could hear the tension in Dad's voice. He didn't care how much the coin was worth. It would end up in a museum, anyway. He wanted to know when it dated from. If it was much before 1610, then it would be strong evidence for contact with Europe before that time.

The collector missed the tense note in Dad's voice. In fact, I think he missed Dad's voice altogether. He kept on talking as if we weren't there. "Very fine condition. Only the graining and the lettering are worn. This is beautiful."

"How old?" Dad leaned over the counter, talking slowly and loudly. I thought he was about to grab the old man by the lapels and shake him into answering.

The collector looked up. "Old? Oh, yes, yes. How old? Let's see now. The lettering is worn. Definitely Elizabeth— see the ER?" He pointed at a couple of letters on either side of the ship's mast. "Trouble is, they didn't put dates on many coins in those days. Makes it more difficult to narrow down." He removed his glasses, reached over, and picked up a magnifying eyepiece that he slowly screwed into his right eye socket. Next he pulled over a desk lamp, adjusted its angle, and brought the coin up to his eye. Automatically Dad and I leaned forward until all three heads were clustered around the coin. I thought Dad was going to explode with the tension.

"What we need is the mint mark," the collector said to

himself. "That would tell us what we need to know. Now, where is it? Aha!" He jerked up, and Dad and I jumped back in surprise. "Here it is! Just as I thought. A sword. Remarkable. I doubt if very many of these were ever minted. It really is a very fine specimen. If you ever consider selling it, I—"

"What date?" Dad almost shouted.

"Oh!" The collector looked flustered. "The sword mint mark wasn't used for very long. Definitely pre-Armada."

Dad let out a long sigh. I wished I'd paid more attention to history lessons.

"When was that?" I asked.

I was rewarded with another of those looks that suggested not knowing when the Armada took place merely confirmed the old man's opinion that I and my entire generation were a total waste of time.

"Don't you know your history, young man?" he asked witheringly. "The Spanish Armada of 1588. Philip II of Spain's attempt to wrest the throne from Elizabeth and make the country Catholic again. Francis Drake playing bowls on the cliffs. Don't they teach you anything these days?"

I didn't feel the question required an answer. In any case, the collector rose from his seat and plucked a book off the shelf behind him.

"For an exact date we'll need to look at this. Ah, yes, the sword mint mark was only used for a short period of time. A few months, in fact, in the spring of 1582."

"Twenty-eight years before Henry Hudson sailed into the bay." Dad looked almost triumphant. Then a frown crossed his face. "How long would something like this have remained in circulation?"

The collector shook his head. "Hard to say. Not long. That's certain in this case. Very few must have been made.

From a numismatic point of view, this was a very interesting time. Henry VIII—Elizabeth's father," he added, looking pointedly at me, "had debased the silver standard and Elizabeth restored it. She also introduced the three-halfpence and three-farthing coins. All in all, I would have to say—"

"But how long?" Dad cut in. "Could they have been in circulation for thirty years?"

"Very unlikely," The old man seemed completely unfazed at being thrown off his explanation. "As I said, there were very few of them. I suspect you'd have been hard-pressed to find one even ten years after they were minted."

Dad focused hard on the collector. "So, it would be unlikely that a sailor in 1610 would have a 1582 angel in his purse?"

"Impossible, I'd say. Even if it had remained in circulation for a long time, the high-value Elizabethan coinage would have been withdrawn when James I assumed the throne in 1603. Monarchs in those days didn't like to have the coins of their predecessors rattling around. Much preferred their own pictures." The collector made a funny dry noise in his throat, which I assumed was a chuckle.

Dad's shoulders relaxed and a faint smile crossed his lips. "Thank you. Thank you very much."

On the way home Dad was talkative. I think he was trying out his theory on me. "This is a pre-Hudson coin. It's unlikely in the extreme that it could have arrived in James Bay through trade. The only English presence was on the Newfoundland coast, and the trade routes didn't run from there to the bay. They ran from the St. Lawrence River north to James Bay. The French were at Quebec by then, but I doubt they would have English coins with them. And even if they did, they wouldn't trade gold with the First Nations. So this coin must have been brought to the area by an English explorer before Henry Hudson."

"I guess so." It seemed reasonable, but then I wasn't an expert. Unfortunately the experts weren't so easily convinced. Dad presented his find to his colleagues at the university as soon as he could. They shouted him down. The idea was too radical, and they were upset that he had gone to a commercial collector instead of the much slower academic route. Dad recognized his mistake.

"I should have taken more time, amassed more evidence to back up my claims. I rushed it too much. Now they're even more fixed in their thinking and I'll never budge them regardless of how much evidence I find."

It always amazed me how difficult it was to convince scientists of something new. I thought they were supposed to have open minds. Anyway, Dad got very depressed. It was just about this time that Mom announced she and I were moving out, so that didn't help. I think Dad had a pretty miserable winter, although he always made an effort to be happy when I was around. The situation wasn't helped when he learned that the archaeology department was cutting back on his fieldwork budget for the summer. Studying pre-Hudson trade routes suddenly wasn't a hot topic.

Dad wasn't one to give up, though, and that was why I was his only assistant back at the James Bay site the second summer. He had financed a lot of the trip himself and had been given some help from the local Cree, who were interested in his work as long as he didn't remove anything sacred or disturb any burials. This time we ignored the midden and spread our search more widely over the camp. Unfortunately we still didn't find much—some trade goods, but nothing as datable as the angel. The only European artifact was a bone button, but that could have come from anywhere at any time.

"It's just a question of collecting as much evidence as possible to build as strong a case as I can," Dad said the night before my canoe trip. "After all, it took Charles Darwin decades to collect enough information to convince people of evolution and, even today, there are those who don't believe him. All I can do is keep searching."

Dad had seemed depressed. I think he had been hoping for something as spectacular as the angel, but that sort of thing only happened once in a lifetime.

His mood had rubbed off on me and contributed to my sleepless night. In any case, I had felt I needed the morning canoe jaunt to blow away all my cobwebs.

I was thinking about all of this as I sat drifting that morning and watching the fog roll toward me. Little did I know that the answer Dad was searching for was in the fog.

The warrior sat by his small fire deep in thought. He was alone and less than a half day's travel from the strangers. His people were camped another day's travel to the south, but he would not go there yet. He had enough with him to trade with the strangers. In his hands he held the frozen water. It reflected the flickering flames of his campfire over which sizzled a small bird on a stick.

Obviously these newcomers needed his help. Their land must indeed be a wondrous place and very different from his land. They knew so little of here, not having small canoes to travel the rivers and lakes in summer or shoes for walking on top of the snow in winter. Many of the visitors looked sick, and even had the black lips that came sometimes after a particularly long and hard winter. He had seen for himself they could not hunt well, and most had the sunken eyes that showed they were near starvation. All these factors would give his people advantages in trade. He thrilled at what magic he might get in exchange for a complete canoe or an entire caribou carcass. But he must be patient. He must make a good trade for the things they had given him and return to show his people. Then he could persuade them to trade for more.

Slowly he put down the frozen water and picked up the knife. He was certain his people could get more of these and probably some of the hatchets he had seen. Maybe, and the warrior in him thrilled at the thought, they could even get one of the long sticks that made noise and brought down game from far away. Then they need never fear attack from their enemies again. It was a good thought: safety for his people and fear spread far among his enemies. Quietly the warrior began to sing a battle song.

It told of a fight long ago when his people had defeated a raiding party of the hated *Iri-akhoiw*. It had happened far to the south at the limits of his people's travels. The *Iri-akhoiw* rarely moved this far north, being partly farmers, but occasionally they followed the great trading circle north in search of prisoners and plunder.

The lot of a prisoner of the *Iri-akhoiw* was not an enviable one. With luck, and if you stood up to the beatings to test your character, you might be selected to be adopted by a family who had recently lost a member. If so, and if you worked hard, you would be accepted. If not, you would be burned with hot coals and sticks, slowly and painfully, from the feet up. Then you would be scalped and hot sand rubbed in the wound. If you fainted, you would be revived with water and food and the process continued because the point was that you should endure as much pain as humanly possible before you died. When at last you did die, your flesh would be ritually eaten so that all the *Iri-akhoiw* could partake of your bravery.

On the occasion that the warrior sang about, this had not happened. The *Kenistenoag* had seen the enemy first, watched carefully, and caught them in the open before they could build one of their stockades. The slaughter had been great and the *Iri-akhoiw* had not returned for many seasons.

Of course, there were many occasions when the outcome had been the other way, and the invaders had fallen upon an unsuspecting village, but it was better to sing of the victories. When the song was done, the warrior crawled into his rough lean-to and huddled beneath his caribou-skin blanket. Tomorrow he would load up his sled, return to the strangers, and make a good trade. Things were turning out well. Content, the warrior slept.

THREE

I felt the chill in the air before the fog actually enveloped me. I was wearing a sweatshirt, but the morning was warm so I just had shorts on. The first thing I noticed was a rash of goose bumps on my legs. I shivered and looked up. The fog was almost on me. It hung like a rolling, heavy curtain over the water a few feet away. Oddly it appeared to be moving toward me unusually fast. In seconds I wouldn't be able to see a thing. Quickly I glanced at the shore to try to get my bearings. I caught a glimpse of a dark line of trees before the shore, the water, the sky, everything, disappeared. It was even hard to make out the bow of the canoe through the smothering fog.

Digging the paddle in hard, I turned the nose of the canoe toward where I had last seen the shore. If I concentrated on keeping even paddle strokes on each side, and was lucky, I should hit the shore and be able to work my way back to camp. If I didn't, I would end up going around in large circles until the fog cleared—not a prospect I relished. Already I was feeling chilled in the damp air.

It was a common misconception that people only got hypothermia in really cold weather. In fact, more people got it in the summer than the winter. It took them by surprise. They went out on the water in T-shirts and shorts and were surprised by how much colder it was on the water than on the shore. Then the weather changed: it clouded over, the wind rose, it began to rain. Next their outboard motors broke down, and they were in real trouble. They were a long way from shore. They hadn't brought any food because they weren't going out for long. Perhaps it was evening and they'd had a couple of beers. They started rowing and built up a sweat. After a few hours of that, they began shivering uncontrollably and got confused, and their hands wouldn't obey them properly. Their core body temperatures dropped below the level of control. They needed external sources of heat in order to warm up. But they didn't have any. They were in the early stages of hypothermia—and it was only August.

I knew the danger I was in. I knew the mistakes I had made: not paying enough attention to the weather, not wearing long pants, not bringing something to eat. But I wasn't too worried. Hypothermia wouldn't be a problem for five or six hours, longer if I didn't overdo it or fall overboard. Surely the sun would burn off this unusual fog long before then. I focused on steady, regular paddling, gazing straight ahead even though I could see nothing but grey beyond the prow. For half an hour I kept this up, hoping I was heading for shore.

Then the fog parted. It didn't roll back in a process reversing the one that had engulfed me, but rather it withdrew all at once. The view shocked me deeply. Wherever I looked, the surface of the bay was dotted with patches of white. They were so unexpected that it took me a minute to realize what they were. Ice floes at the beginning of September, especially after the hot summer we'd had, were impossible. Yet there they were. I stopped paddling. As I did, my eye was drawn from the ice floes to an even weirder view. The fog was still thinning, but now it seemed to draw in on itself at a point in front of the canoe. As it did, it gave the impression that it was thickening and solidifying into the shape of a ship.

It had to be a trick of the light. I closed my eyes and shook my head to dispel the illusion. But when I opened my eyes, there was the ship, solid now, sitting on the calm water about a hundred metres in front of me. It was perhaps twenty-five metres from bow to stern, high at the front and back and with three masts from which sails hung, billowed only slightly in the light breeze.

I could just make out the gold lettering on the stern—*Discovery*. Beside the ship and tied to it was a low rowboat with a single, short mast. Both vessels had a grey, washed-out look.

My first reaction was fear at the almost ghostly appearance of the scene, and a shiver ran down my spine. I looked around. The fog had withdrawn and lay like a curtain around me. Within the circle of fog the air was clear and the sun shone in a blue sky. The sea was calm, and the ice glinted at me mischievously in the sunlight.

I returned my gaze to the ship. Oddly, although the breeze was catching the ship's sails and must be moving it along, and I had ceased to paddle so was only drifting, the distance between the canoe and the ship hadn't altered.

Was the scene real? The vessel certainly wasn't one I expected to encounter here. This was no fishing boat or a late-season tourist boat. But then boaters were sometimes an eccentric lot. Irrationally my mind jumped back to my trip out to the West Coast with Mom. In Nanaimo's harbour we had seen all manner of strangely rigged craft, from 1920s rum runners and lovingly polished, sleek wooden yachts to a complete replica of a Chinese junk. Some had been all over the Pacific, and one had even sailed through the Northwest Passage. This craft must be the lovingly re-created toy of a rich mariner cruising the bay for summer fun. Even as I thought this, I knew it wasn't true. This was no ordinary ship, no expensive fantasy of a wealthy seagoing history buff. This was a ghost ship.

My rational mind rejected the idea of ghosts, but deep inside I knew that was what I was witnessing. I felt a rising panic, and yet I was as cold and immobile as the ice that surrounded me. I could no more have removed my gaze from the scene before me than flown in the air.

As I watched, spellbound, I noticed there were people moving on the ship and in the boat. I heard a deep, rich voice carry over the distance between us.

"Stand aside," it said firmly. "I would go with the captain."

"Thou need not, Master Carpenter," another voice spoke. "I have nought against thee. The captain has used thee as unfairly as the rest, and I would have use of thy skills on the journey home."

"Your journey is but to the gallows, Juet, and your home but a traitor's grave," the deep voice continued. "Now stand aside while I load my chest and fowling piece."

There was a flurry of activity on the deck of the larger vessel, and a chest and some other objects were passed down into the boat. They were followed by the figure of a man climbing down a rope ladder. He settled himself in the boat, then shouted back up, "Prickett! Leave some token at the Capes of the Furious Overfall where the fowls breed so that we may know you have been there."

"Aye, I shall," a third voice responded.

Then a high-pitched voice joined in. "Prickett, beware of

Juet and keep your writings for our record."

"Aye. I shall, but 'tis Greene who commands now."

"Beware that devil, too," the high voice continued. "He will sit at your table and eat your bread before he stabs you in the back."

"Enough talk," Juet's voice cut over the others. "Cut them loose and we be on our way.

There was activity on the deck and a length of rope snaked down into the small boat. Almost immediately the larger vessel pulled away. A figure leaned over the railing at the back.

"Now we shall feast on the food thou hast hoarded and sail home safe. May thy bones freeze in the ice of this godforsaken land. Thou shalt endanger the lives of no more stout sailors with thy lunatic schemes of the Orient. There be no passage to the Spice Lands through this barren place. 'Tis but death thy madness brings upon thee, Henry Hudson."

There was no reply from the boat and, as the distance between the two increased, the fog rolled back, blocking the scene from my view. The familiar grey wall surrounded me once more.

For a long time I gazed at the grey curtain. I knew what I had seen—the ghosts of men who had died centuries before. The old-fashioned ship wasn't a replica; it was the real thing—the *Discovery*! The ship in which Henry Hudson had sailed these waters in 1610 and 1611 and from which his crew had set him adrift to die a lonely death on the shores of the bay that would always bear his name. Somehow I had witnessed him being cast adrift. The man with the deep voice, Philip Staffe the carpenter, had been the only one who voluntarily went with his captain to share his fate.

I sat motionless, shivering. Ghosts! Could I have the disorientation of hypothermia already? No. I had been on the water no more than an hour and, although there was a chill in the air, my core body temperature was a long way from dropping seriously. There must be a rational explanation. Then a more pressing consequence than my confusion sprang into my mind. I had no idea which way I was facing. Before the encounter I was fairly sure I was headed more or less toward shore. Now, after drifting and not paying attention, I might be headed straight into the wild, open waters of Hudson Bay. However, any activity was better than doing nothing. I began paddling toward what I hoped was safety.

Confidently the warrior laid out his trade goods before Hairy Face—two beaver pelts and two caribou skins. From the pouch beneath his arm he took out the items he had been given the day before. On one of the beaver pelts he laid the knife. On the other, the frozen water and the trinkets. Then he replaced the things, handed the beaver skins over, and stood. This would be a good trade.

Hairy Face did not look happy, but he nodded and handed the skins to those behind him. Then he produced a hatchet and laid it on the ground. The warrior was excited, but did not show it. Slowly he took one of the caribou skins and placed it next to the hatchet. Hairy Face shook his head and indicated the other skin, as well. This was too much. This was not a good trade. Caribou skins were much more valuable than beaver; they could be turned into everything from clothes and blankets to tents. The warrior shook his head. He pointed to the hatchet and raised two fingers—two hatchets were worth two caribou skins. Again Hairy Face shook his head. He pointed at the hatchet and held up one finger, then at the caribou skins and held up two.

The warrior had a problem. The more he could take back, the easier it would be to convince his people there were benefits to be had from contact with these strangers. A bad trade would make that more difficult. On the other hand, Hairy Face might call off the trade altogether if he was unhappy with it. The warrior had to have something. Reluctantly he added the other caribou skin to the trade pile and took the hatchet.

Hairy Face stood and smiled. As on the day before, he made eating gestures. Perhaps he wanted to trade for food. The warrior would remember that next time, but now he must return and convince his people he had done a good thing. Making the gesture for sleep, the warrior indicated he would return in five days and trade again. Then he turned and walked into the trees.

Overall, the warrior was happy. The two caribou skins for one hatchet still annoyed him. He had thought the trading would be easy because these strangers were so obviously poor at looking after themselves, but he had been wrong. Still, he had made contact and begun trade. If he could persuade his people to continue, only good could come of it.

FOUR

The first thing I heard was the sound of oars slicing the water. It was coming from close by and over to my right. I stopped paddling and listened. Then I heard the voice. It was high-pitched—the voice of Henry Hudson

"Keep to it, men. The shore can be not far now."

"Aye," the deep voice of Philip Staffe said. "If we could but perceive it through this damnable mist."

"Be of stout heart, Master Staffe," Hudson continued. "The Lord will see to our needs if we have but faith."

"That may be, but I have yet to see the evidence of it. We are a sickly crew and cannot hope to prosper for long in these inhospitable climes. Had we but set ourselves to the task of following the *Discovery*, we might be near the Furious Overfall by now."

"And then what?" Hudson asked. "Do you expect that with our sickness and want of supplies we could navigate such a treacherous stretch of water and then sail this shallop all the way back to St. Katherine's Pool? Philip, our only hope lies in

Jack's idea of enlisting the help of the local salvages and making a contact with the French at Quebec or the salvage city of Hochelaga."

"Aye." A third voice joined the conversation, younger and softer than the others. "The salvages know both of the water on which we sit and the communities of the Frenchmen. Surely there is trade and we need simply follow the routes of the goods to find succour."

"May be, Jack. May be. Yet I—"

Staffe's voice was cut off by my appearance out of the fog. What I saw was the bow of a boat arching above my small canoe. It was heading straight for the side. If it hit, it would stave in the canoe and I would end up in the water. Not a prospect I relished.

Frantically I dug the paddle in deep and pulled to turn away from the collision. My best chance was to swing around parallel to the boat and, hopefully, pass alongside it. The canoe was much more manoeuvrable than the rowboat and responded quickly, but the crew of the boat were working, too. With much shouting and pulling on the oars, they were bringing their bow around, fortunately in the same direction as me. It seemed we would avoid a collision, but only just. I looked up. Five faces peered at me over the gunwales. They were very close, unusually pale, and colourless. The boat, the faces, the rough clothing the men wore, everything, was a uniform grey, as if made from the fog itself.

We were very close now and passing each other in opposite directions at quite a speed. They were as silent as I. One of the faces in particular caught my eye. It belonged to a boy, not much older than I. He had dark hair, long and lying over his neck, and his features were well formed and open. His eyes, despite the lack of colour, seemed to sparkle with life and fun. As I gazed at him, his face broke into a smile.

Encouraged, I was about to say something when a shadow appeared at the edge of my vision. I turned. One of the figures farther down the boat had an oar. He had lifted it from the water in the manoeuvre to turn, but kept it held out horizontally. It was approaching my head at a frightening speed. With not even time to duck, I closed my eyes against the imminent pain. There was none. Only a cold, clammy burst of air sweeping over my face, then nothing. I opened my eyes and turned. The strange boat was already past me, becoming part of the surrounding fog.

"Wait!" I shouted instinctively, but it was no use. As suddenly as it had appeared, the boat vanished and the grey curtain swept around me once more. The only thing I was left with was the final echo of the deep voice.

"In troth, the salvages hereabouts speak the English of King James."

Then I was alone once more. Alone and scared. I shivered. How many ghostly scenes of the long-dead past were floating in this unearthly fog?

Nervously I looked around. There was nothing, but I couldn't get rid of the unpleasant feeling there was someone just out of sight. My stressed mind began to imagine hordes of dead sailors everywhere, ready to materialize out of the fog and terrorize me. I had to get out of there. In a panic I grabbed the paddle and began working furiously. I didn't care where I was going or that the sweat I was building up would only hasten the onset of hypothermia. I had to escape.

In an insanity of activity I paddled wildly, spraying water all about with my poorly executed strokes. The bow of the canoe swung crazily from side to side as I dug the paddle in frantically, first on one side, then on the other, heedless of whether I was heading toward the shore or out into the bay.

I had no idea how long I worked, but I was exhausted and

drenched in sweat when the fog suddenly cleared. I didn't see it go; it was simply there one minute and not the next.

The surprisingly bright sunlight made me screw up my eyes, and that was why I didn't see the rock until it was too late. It wasn't big, but it was sharp-edged and I was paddling hard. With a sickening crunch the rock gouged a long, jagged hole in the fibreglass bottom of the canoe. Cold water instantly began pouring in. Fortunately the first thing I saw when the collision jerked my eyes back open was the shore. It was rocky, inhospitable, and backed by a line of unwelcoming dark trees. Nonetheless, it was dry land and only a few metres in front of me. With a few last paddle strokes, as the water continued to pour in, I pushed the now-heavy canoe toward safety.

With a grumbling noise the canoe grounded on the sloping shore. Hurriedly I stepped into knee-deep water. The shock of the cold made me gasp, but I kept working, grabbing the canoe and dragging it onto the beach as far above the water line as I could. Then I slumped beside it, exhausted and con-fused. Almost immediately, and despite the bright sun, I began to shiver. Partly it was the sweat cooling on my body, partly it was my chilled legs, but mostly it was reaction to the impossibilities I had seen. To stop myself thinking, I took stock of my surroundings. I could worry about why there were ghosts later.

There was no sign of fog anywhere. As far as I could see, the water before me was clear and calm. On the horizon I could barely make out the dark line of an island out in the bay. With relief I noticed there were no ice floes in sight. The beach itself was composed of sharp limestone boulders. In both directions it stretched off with only an occasional washed-up tree trunk to break the monotony. The beach was narrow and the trees behind it closely packed and dark.

Moving forward, I examined the damage to the canoe. The hole was jagged and almost a half metre long. There was no way the canoe was going anywhere without extensive repairs. How could I have been so stupid, paddling about wildly because of some imagined ghosts? That was what they must have been. Ghosts didn't exist, so I must have imagined them. They were tricks of the fog magnified by my worried state. Maybe I had even dozed off for a few minutes and dreamt it all. Dad would be worrying by now.

Before the fog enshrouded me I had been paddling north, with the eastern shore of James Bay to my right. If I kept the landward side of the beach to my left and walked, sooner or later I would arrive back at camp.

I knew you weren't supposed to leave the sight of a crash in the wilderness, but it would be a long time before Dad called for serious help and I figured the camp couldn't be far. The activity would help keep me warm and I would probably be back before the floatplane arrived in the afternoon. Then we could come and get the canoe. If it was farther than I thought and the floatplane came looking for me, I would be easy to spot on the beach.

Stopping only long enough to pull the canoe a little farther from the water, I set off. I knew that by concentrating on the present I wouldn't have to think about the past, either my recent past or the one I had apparently witnessed. I figured I had it all worked out, but I was wrong. The past still had some surprises in store for me before I got home.

➤

"No!" The anger in the *okimah*'s voice shocked the warrior into silence. "We will not trade with these *kawaaposit* who come uninvited into our land. They respect nothing of the earth and only bad will come of it."

The *okimah* was the senior elder and speechmaker of the band. He and the warrior were sitting with the other men around a fire in the centre of the collection of skin tents that housed their people. Others hovered around on the edge of the firelight. Anyone could speak their mind, and several had done so on both sides of the argument, but it was the talk between the *okimah* and the warrior that would determine what was to be done.

"It is true what you say," the warrior spoke quietly. "These *kawaaposit* know nothing of the land. This is an abundant winter, yet they starve. But they are not *natuwewak*, not threatening strangers. I think they would offer us no harm and we can get much of benefit in trade with them." In a dramatic gesture he held up the hatchet and knife he had brought back. Raising his voice to address the surrounding crowd, he continued. "With enough of these, and even with the sticks that kill with noise, we need never fear our enemies again. They would fear us."

A sigh of agreement passed around the circle. To live without fear, that would be something worth trading for. The noise died away as the *okimah* began speaking again.

"Yes, that would indeed be good, but would we truly live without fear? Trade goes two ways, and we have seen that these strangers are traders. Two caribou skins for a single hatchet is not a good trade." The warrior flinched. He knew it was not a good trade, and he could hear murmurs of agreement from the crowd. He had lost a point in the argument.

"But to trade for the wonders we see here," the *okimah* continued, "we must give something the strangers want. That is the nature of trade. We know these *kawaaposit* come from far away, but we do not know how many there are of them. Perhaps there are many, like the rocks on the beach. If our enemies need to fear us with the strangers' weapons, need we not fear these strangers themselves?"

"They are only a few in one canoe," the warrior interrupted, "and they are sick and hungry. We could easily kill them all if we wished."

"Let us not talk of killing. They have not attacked us. Nevertheless, where some come, others may follow, and they may not be sick and hungry. If they see benefit to trade with us, they will surely come in their big canoes with wings. And note this, too. If there is benefit for them in trading with us, will there not also be benefit for them in trading with our enemies?"

A worried murmur swept through the crowd. Sensing the people were swinging to his way of thinking, the *okimah* continued before the warrior could say anything. "If our enemies need fear us with the weapons of these strangers, should we not fear our enemies twice as much if they have the weapons?"

The noise of the crowd swelled.

"I say," the *okimah* said, his voice rising against the increased background noise, "that we should have no contact with these *kawaaposit*. If they starve, it will not be our concern. If they return home, they will have nothing in trade and no reason to bother us again."

The crowd now openly agreed with the *okimah*. The warrior had no more arguments to give. He had lost. Perhaps it was for the best. He would not return to the strangers' camp.

FIVE

It was good to be walking and I soon warmed up. The beach was clear and the going easy. The only problem was that I couldn't stop my mind from working. Like a dog worrying a bone, it kept going over what I had seen. It even seemed to make an odd kind of sense.

I knew something of Henry Hudson from a project I'd done for social studies in school, and I had even read a book about him. It had been the only thing I could find in the library and had been old-fashioned but quite interesting. It was based on a journal kept by one of Hudson's crew. The crewman had such an unlikely name that I still remembered it—Abacuck Prickett. I figured things were different four hundred years ago, but I still had trouble imagining going through life with a handle like that.

Hudson had left London in 1610 to search for the Northwest Passage to the Orient. It was his fourth voyage. Previously he had explored a possible Northeast Passage around the north of Russia and sailed up what was now the

Hudson River in New York. This time he was convinced he knew the answer and a year or two would see him returning home with a shipload of valuable spices.

With Hudson sailed his son, John, who had been on his earlier voyages, and several men who had sailed with him before. Among them was the mate, Robert Juet, with whom Hudson had quarrelled before, and a friend, Henry Greene, who had been staying at Hudson's house.

After exploring Ungava Bay, Hudson's ship made a perilous passage of Hudson Strait, which had been named the Furious Overfall by the explorer John Davis when he had seen huge pieces of ice rushing through it in 1587. When Hudson reached the large body of water beyond, he was convinced he was within reach of Japan. He was horribly disappointed when, after sailing down the eastern shore of Hudson Bay, he ended up in James Bay and was faced with a western shore blocking his way. Since it was too late in the season to return, the ship's crew settled in for the winter.

It was a hard time, with scurvy running rampant and only minimal contact with the local First Nations. One man died. When the ice finally released the ship in June 1611, the sick and weakened crew were desperate to head home before what little food they had left ran out. Hudson, on the other hand, wanted to continue exploring and sailed aimlessly around James Bay.

This was too much, and the crew, led by Juet and Greene, cast Hudson, his son, Staffe, and the sickest of the rest adrift to die in one of the ship's boats. No one ever discovered what happened to them.

The saga of Henry Hudson was one of murder and mystery, and it fascinated me. Was Hudson a poor leader who couldn't control his crew, or were the crew a bunch of hardened villains? Why did Hudson take Juet with him? Juet was, after all, a man who had led a mutiny against Hudson on a previous occasion. Why did he take Greene, someone who had to be sneaked aboard at Gravesend, was not on the crew list, and was to be paid directly from Hudson's pocket? What did happen to Hudson's lonely boat after it was cast adrift?

All these questions came flooding back to me as I went over the visions I had recently witnessed. Despite my skepticism and my fear of ghosts, I was in little doubt that what I had witnessed had been images of events that had occurred in 1611. The specific presence of Juet, Greene, Staffe, and Prickett proved it. I was less sure whether I had watched a ghostly reenactment played out in some supernatural fog, or whether my overstressed mind had created hallucinations based on what I had read years before. Either way it was a disturbing series of events. Did ghosts really exist, or was I going crazy? At least now the fog had lifted and the world, in the bright morning sunlight, had returned to normal.

I was so wrapped up in my thoughts and worries that I almost fell over the figure sitting on the beach. It had its back to me and was gazing out to sea, as preoccupied with its thoughts as I was with mine. Whoever it was must be a member of the local First Nations and must have a boat or all-terrain vehicle close by. Maybe I could scrounge a ride back to Dad's camp. I put on my friendliest smile. "Hello," I said cheerfully.

Startled by my voice, the figure leaped to its feet and turned to face me. My smile died. The cold horrors of the fog rushed back over me. I knew this face. It was thinner than I remembered it—painfully thin—and the eyes, surrounded by dark shadows were sunk deep into their sockets. But they still had the sparkle I remembered. It was the boy who had smiled at me from the ghostly rowboat as we passed in the fog.

Everything I had planned to say vanished from my mind. "You!" was all I could gasp.

"Aye," the boy replied, "and 'tis you, the salvage from the small boat."

"Salvage?" I asked.

"Aye," he repeated, "*sauvage*, as the French say, man of the woods, native of these parts. Yet you look not like the others we have seen." A frown crossed his face. "And you speak the king's English passably well. How can this be?"

I ignored his question and asked one of my own, even though I dreaded the answer. "What's your name?"

"I am named John," he said, stepping forward and holding out his hand. "But most call me Jack."

"And your other name?" I ignored the outstretched hand. "What's your family name?"

The puzzled look returned. "Why, Hudson."

"And your father is Henry Hudson, the explorer?" I had to be certain.

"Aye," he responded proudly, "a great explorer. Greater than Willoughby, Davis, or Frobisher. But how know you such things?"

Again I ignored his question. Retreating, I sat heavily on the beach. The nightmare hadn't ended. The fog had gone and there was colour in this world now, but it wasn't my world. Or not his. One of us was wrong.

"What year is this?" I asked.

John Hudson still stood with his hand held out, looking down at me. "The year of our Lord 1611. As close I can calculate, around the middle of the month of August."

The middle of August 1611. My mind rebelled. "No!" I almost shouted. "It's Saturday, the first of September, 2001."

"Well," he continued calmly, "Saturday it may well be. I might even allow for it being nearer the month of September than my calculations, but even with the uncertainties of our calendar in the dire straits we find ourselves, it is most definitely the year 1611." His face brightened at a new thought. "But you keep not the same calendar as us, being in no way Christian. Are you one of the Lost Tribes of Israel?"

"No," I replied in confusion. "I'm Christian. United Church. It *is* the year 2001 after the birth of Christ."

John Hudson finally withdrew his hand and hunkered down on the rocks beside me. "This is passably strange," he said thoughtfully. "It cannot be both 1611 and 2001. Yet we are both convinced of our own facts. This is truly a most unusual land we have come to visit."

My fear had diminished as we sat talking, apparently normally, on the reassuringly uncomfortable stones of the beach. Then I remembered the oar that had hit, yet not hit, my head. I had to find something out.

"My name is Alfred Lister," I said, holding my hand out, "but my friends call me Al."

"Well, Alfred. I am much pleased to make your acquaintance, despite the strange circumstances of it."

He reached out and took my hand in his. I tensed, half expecting nothing but a cold draft as we touched, but it was an ordinary handshake. My companion's hand was skinny, and I could feel the bones when I gripped it, but the skin felt warm and alive and his grip was firm. I returned the smile that now wreathed his pale face. I didn't have the slightest idea what was happening, but at least knowing the figure before me was solid and not a wraith comforted me a bit.

"However this has come about," he continued, "will you come, Alfred, to our meagre camp and meet my father and the others? It is not far."

I wasn't sure. A short while ago I had been happily walking along the beach toward *my* father's camp. Now I was being invited to visit another camp that had existed almost four hundred years before I was even born! It was insane. But what choice did I have? Either John Hudson had travelled in time and his camp wouldn't exist and we could proceed on to mine, or I had travelled in time and there would be little point in trying to find my father. In any case, I instinctively liked this strange boy. Despite the apparent impossibility of our meeting and his odd way of speaking, I felt at ease with him. The possibility that he existed in my time but was subject to insane delusions crossed my mind, but I dismissed it. It couldn't explain the happenings in the fog, and my new friend seemed completely sane.

"All right," I replied. "I'd like to visit your camp. But on the condition that you call me Al."

Hudson laughed. "I see you like not your given name. Very well, Al it shall be. But in your turn, you must address me as Jack. There is nought remiss with John, yet all address me as Jack since, as a stripling, I ascended without fear a tall oak in the manner of the old tale of the giant killer and the beanstalk."

"Okay," I said, unable to stop smiling at the happy chatter of my companion. "I'll call you Jack."

Standing, Jack Hudson led the way along the beach. Despite the disorientation I felt at the impossible events of the morning, a part of me hoped it was really happening. Perhaps, somehow, I had really travelled in time. As I followed the figure into the unknown, I couldn't help feeling this was a much better way to find out about the past than rooting around in ancient garbage piles. What would Dad give to be wherever I was right now? I was on my way to meet Henry Hudson, famous explorer and the subject of four centuries of speculation. It might be impossible, but it was certainly exciting.

Again the warrior was watching an intruder in his land, but this time there was just one of them. It was high summer, and the warrior had come to the shore to fish. Fortunately he had seen the seated figure first.

It was one of the strangers from the winter. He looked hungry and sat looking out over the great water. The warrior was confused. He had watched the strangers leave in their winged canoe soon after the ice had broken. That had been almost two cycles of the moon ago. Why had this one returned? Where were his companions? Where was the winged canoe? What did the return mean?

As he observed, a second figure approached from the north. This was one the warrior did not recognize. He was dressed differently, in short leggings and a tight shirt, and seemed hardly aware of the world around him. In fact, he almost fell over the first figure. Then the two began talking in their odd tongue and set off along the beach.

The warrior followed, paralleling the beach yet hidden by the undergrowth. At times the newcomer appeared to suspect his presence and nervously scanned the trees. Once, he stared directly at the warrior for some time. But the warrior was too skilled in bushcraft to allow himself to be seen, especially by someone who obviously did not make the forest his home.

The stream where the fish were good was not far. There was a clearing there the warrior would have to cross before the strangers arrived if he was to avoid being seen. Lengthening his stride, the warrior increased his pace through the trees and soon left the two figures on the beach behind. But there was a surprise awaiting him at the clearing. Instead of an open space he could cross quickly, there was a camp. A crude shelter sat in the middle of the clearing and a long wreath of smoke rose from a fire pit in front of it. It was obviously the work of the strangers; none of his people would be so careless or untidy. Yet there was still no sign of the winged ship. One of the smaller canoes was pulled up on the beach, but that was all.

As the warrior watched, the first two figures arrived. One of them shouted something. In response Hairy Face emerged from the shelter. He looked even hungrier than the boy. The warrior was extremely puzzled. Obviously there were not as many strangers here as had been at the winter camp and obviously they were in some distress. What had happened? Had the large canoe been wrecked?

The warrior would not approach the strangers again, but he would watch. Watch and wait until he had answers to some of his questions.

SIX

Silently I followed Jack along the beach. Now I had a chance to observe him. He was about my height and, as far as I could guess, my age. He looked weak but walked strongly, although he stumbled occasionally on the uneven rocks of the beach. He was wearing a loose, grey, three-quarter-length woollen jacket, pulled in by a broad leather belt. A knife was tucked through the belt in the middle of his back, and a small leather pouch dangled over his right hip. His trousers were baggy and dark red. They were pulled tight about his legs just below his knees. He was wearing long stockings that disappeared beneath his trousers and soft, shapeless leather shoes. On his head was a woollen cap of the same red as his trousers, from beneath which his dark hair hung in an unruly mat. His clothing looked comfortable but very old-fashioned.

We walked for about ten minutes, both lost in our own thoughts. Gradually an unsettling feeling that we were being watched grew in my mind. It was similar to the sensation I'd had in the fog. Then there had been ghosts all around me, but this time it seemed that someone, or something, in the trees was watching Jack and me. I kept glancing over but could see nothing suspicious, just the trees and the dark spaces between them. Jack appeared not to be bothered, and that helped me fight the urge to break into a run.

Eventually we came to a clearing by the beach. I recognized the place. My father's camp at the big rock lay a long way to the south. Apparently I had paddled a lot farther north than I had thought.

A sluggish stream flowed across the clearing. Beside it, a boat was drawn up on the shore—the one I had seen in the fog. The ground to my left was rocky with occasional patches of grass and a few stunted trees. On a low rock outcrop a rude shelter had been constructed. It was square, measured about three metres on each side, and was high enough for a short man to stand upright in. The walls were constructed of roughly cut saplings interwoven with branches. The roof appeared to be of similar construction. It looked sturdy enough, but I doubted it would keep out much wind or rain. A small fire pit in the doorway sent up a long wisp of smoke.

Farther away, on the flat ground in front of the rock out-crop, was a larger fire pit with boulders arranged in a semi-circle around it. On the other side of the clearing, two crude crosses stood above mounds of rock, which I assumed with a shudder were graves.

I hesitated in confusion, but Jack didn't stop. Without breaking stride he walked toward the hut. "Father!" he called.

A figure emerged, stooping to negotiate the makeshift doorway. Despite the sun, he was dressed in a long dark blue coat with a thick fur collar. The coat was cinched by a leather belt that also held a long-bladed knife. On the man's head was a wool cap similar to Jack's but with long ear flaps on either side. As he stood, I got a good look at his face. It seemed even more starved than John's. The sunken eyes and prominent cheekbones highlighted what was already a long, thin face. The skin was weather-beaten and wrinkled, and grey hair straggled from beneath his cap. A matching grey beard covered his cheeks and chin. The eyes were the same pale blue as his son's, yet the sparkle was missing. They looked haunted.

"Ah, Jack," the man said as he came forward, "Staffe and Wydhowse have gone hunting, and I would talk with you before their return. What would be—" The man stopped in mid-sentence as his gaze fell on me.

In the pause Jack took the opportunity to speak. Half turning, he waved his arm in my direction. "I have found a companion. He is not like the salvages we have seen and has an odd sense of the year. Yet he professes to the Christian faith, speaks a version of English, and may be of use in our predicament. He goes by the name of Al." With a smile Jack gestured to the bearded man. "Al," he said, "this is my father, the explorer Henry Hudson."

For a moment we regarded each other carefully. Then Hudson stepped forward and held out his hand. "How do you do Master Al? I am much honoured to make your acquaintance."

I moved forward and took his hand. "I am pleased to meet you, Mr. Hudson," I said formally. "I've heard a lot about you."

Almost instantly I realized my mistake. Hudson withdrew his hand and stepped back, shock on his face. "How can this be? Are you, too, a lost voyager from England?"

"No," I replied, wondering how I was going to explain to Henry Hudson circumstances I couldn't even explain to myself. "I'm from the south. Ottawa," I added rather pointlessly.

"How then is it," Hudson continued, "that you are, as Jack says, Christian, know the king's English, and have heard tell of me?"

There was no sane answer to these questions. I could

hardly tell this man I had studied him for a school project almost four hundred years after he died! I kept my answers as vague as I could.

"Where I'm from," I said cautiously, "we take a great interest in the world. People travel all over and report back what they see." It was weak, but easier than trying to explain television, cell phones, and the Internet. It would do for the moment, and it appeared to make sense to Hudson, who nodded understandingly.

"Then you are a nation of travellers and traders," he said thoughtfully, "much like the Portuguese and the Genoese."

It was my turn to nod. If I could keep my responses vague and let Hudson make assumptions that fitted me into his world, it would give me time to think.

A frown crossed Hudson's face. "How is it then that I have not heard of your people? By what name do you call yourselves?"

"Canadians," I answered.

"And where is this Ottawa of which you speak? Is it near to New France?"

New France! Where was that? I searched my mind for what had been happening in Canada in the early 1600s. Wasn't that when Champlain was exploring and setting up a settlement at Quebec City? I decided to chance dropping a name.

"It is to the west of Champlain's settlement at Quebec," I said.

The effect on Jack was electrifying. He jumped forward and said excitedly, "You know of the French. And you have travelled here. There must therefore be a route we might follow to this Quebec to seek succour." He turned from me to his father. "See, this is a sign. It is possible. We must march south if we are to survive."

"Aye!" a new voice joined us. "It is surely a sign."

Looking past Hudson, I saw a gaunt figure emerge from the hut. The man was small and looked deathly ill. He held on to one of the upright doorposts for support. His voice was almost a whine and grated on my ears.

"A sign of the Devil," he continued, "come to tempt us into the wilderness. We must trust to God's mercy. Succour will find us if we but keep faith."

"Syracke Fanner," Hudson said, turning to address the man, "I think not that this boy is the Devil nor in league with the hellish hosts. I think he is but of an unknown tribe—one of the many wonders of this land—and it may be that, if he is to be our salvation, he has been sent by the Lord God himself."

Syracke Fanner stood away from the post and took a few faltering steps toward us. I noticed that he was lame and favoured his right leg heavily. Despite his difficulties, he raised his arm and pointed at me.

"The Devil can take many forms and need not show us his cloven hoof. The Lord God provided manna for his followers as they were starving in the desert. So, too, shall he provide for our wants in this extremity. Our faith is being tested. We must not be found wanting."

"Wanting we shall not be, tonight at least." It was the deep voice from the fog, and it belonged to a tall man who strode purposefully around the side of the hut. "Wydhowse and I have had some of the Lord's luck and bring some meagre sustenance for our evening repast." In one hand Staffe carried an ancient-looking musket. The other held a pole that rested on his shoulder and from which hung two grouse.

"Fanner," Staffe continued, dominating the gathering, "I would hear no more of your Godly whining. We will perish or not by our own efforts and through any help we may enlist. If we sit and wait for your salvation, we will be corpses before the first snow falls." The man's eyes turned to me. "And who is this strangely dressed lad? He looks not like a salvage, but then there is much we know not of this place."

"His name is Al," Jack said, stepping forward. "He comes from the south, close by to New France, yet he speaks English."

"Does he indeed." The owner of the deep voice placed his musket and kill on the ground and approached. "Well, then, I suspect you may be a timely addition to our small party." He held out a large, gnarled hand. "I am Philip Staffe, carpenter to this sorry band, and the only loyal servant of Master Hudson here. Will you join us in our repast?"

"I will, thank you," I said hesitantly as my hand was engulfed in Staffe's mitt.

"Very well," Staffe continued. "And now I must return and bring Wydhowse in. He rests in the woods, being exhausted by our exertions."

Staffe turned and strode back the way he had come. A silence fell. His presence had dominated us all, and we seemed less without him. It was Hudson who eventually spoke.

"Syracke," he said, turning to the lame man, "we will do nothing without discussion and you shall have your say then as shall we all." Turning to Jack, he continued. "Jack, settle our new friend by the fire and prepare the beasts Staffe has provided. Our decisions will be easier made with some food in our bellies. I will return Syracke to his cot."

Taking the lame man gently by the arm, Hudson helped him back into the hut. Jack ushered me onto a rock by the low fire and retrieved the grouse from where Staffe had laid them.

"Can you clean the entrails from these?" he asked, placing the bounty before me and offering me his knife. "Take care that you waste none, for we can make a passable soup from the skin and the innards." My shocked expression must have betrayed me, because he continued. "Two small birds are little enough for six of us, and it is the first success at the hunt for

a week past. We must get what goodness we can from nature's
meagre bounty. Save, too, the feathers. We may yet come to
boiling what good we can from them."

"Yes," I replied, horrified at the calm way Jack described
the desperate situation his party was in. I was glad, though,
of the wilderness experiences I'd had with Dad. Cleaning and
skinning would be no problem. Perhaps I could even rig some
snares and help with the hunt. But could I? How long was I
going to stay here? How much time was passing in the real
world? With all these worries spinning in my head, I took the
knife and got to work.

Jack collected wood and built up the fire. At least if I kept
my hands and mind busy, I wouldn't have a chance to think
about my situation. I suspected that way led to insanity and
was glad for the easy acceptance I had found among these
characters cast adrift in a world so full of wonders that one
more made little difference.

I worked busily cleaning, plucking, and skinning. What I
would normally have thrown away, I dropped in a large iron
pot by my side. As the fire grew, Jack went to collect more
fuel. Staffe returned, supporting Wydhowse, who looked
almost unconscious. With hardly even a look in my direction,
he slumped by the fire and appeared to fall asleep.

I was so wrapped up in my thoughts and my work that I
hardly noticed it was getting dark. Eventually I couldn't
ignore it and looked up. The sun was low in the sky, and the
few clouds were tinged orange and pink. It was going to be a
pretty sunset. Then I almost dropped the grouse I was holding.
It shouldn't be sunset. It should barely be lunchtime, let alone
late in a northern summer evening.

Oddly the fact that I was ten or twelve hours out of my
own time was more disturbing than the realization I was four
hundred years adrift. Somehow I could more easily accept I

had come face-to-face with a long-dead explorer than that I had lived through a single day too quickly. I shook my head. Tears of utter helplessness were close to the surface. I felt lost and out of control. Where was I? When was I? What was I doing here? How did I get here? How would I get back?

My self-pity was interrupted by Jack's arrival with several sharpened sticks. He began dividing the birds and skewering the pieces on the sticks. "My hunger is so great," he said, smiling, at me, "that I would eat one of these fowl uncooked, feathers and all. But mayhap we should cook them to some degree to increase their attraction to our palates. What say you, Al?"

I returned Jack's smile and held up my bloodied hands. "I think I should go and wash up before I eat anything."

Rising, I walked toward the stream. The cold water felt good on my hands and arms. I splashed some on my face and was about to drink from my cupped hands when I felt an uncomfortable itching in the centre of my back. It was accompanied by the certainty that someone was again watching me. Abruptly I spun around, splashing water on the ground. There was no one there. My back had been to the trees, and all I could see were dark shadows. I strained my eyes, but there was only what there should have been: trees, bushes, rocks, and the long shadows produced by the sinking sun.

I looked back at the fire. Other figures had gathered around, and I could hear several voices in conversation. For all their unaccountable strangeness, the small party looked very inviting just then. And what was my alternative? I had travelled in time. Impossible though it seemed, I had to admit there was no other way to explain the events of the day. My only choices were to return to the fire and see what this mysterious adventure still had in store for me, or face the dark terrors of fleeing alone into the woods. Even were I to flee I would probably still be lost in time, with the added circumstance of being alone. And after my feelings of being watched from the darkness, I didn't relish that prospect. With a last look at the silent woods, I made my way back to the fire.

The warrior crouched on the bank of the stream, so close to the new stranger that he could have hit him easily with a thrown pebble. He could see it was only a boy, crouched by the river and washing his hands and face. The paleness of his skin was quite remarkable, even more so than the strangers who had wintered in camp. By the reactions of the hairy-faced leader and the tall hunter, this boy, even though he could speak the language of the strangers, was not a part of the group. He seemed uncomfortable and was treated as an outsider by the others. He was also plump and well fed, unlike the others who were obviously starving. Yet the newcomer had made no attempt to trade and appeared to have no possessions with him. Where had he come from and where was his canoe?

In all the time he had been watching, the warrior had been working over this new puzzle, yet he could think of no answer. The strangers were going to die. There was no doubt about that. Two of them were already close to the other world. This was the easiest time of year. Fish, birds, deer, and berries were abundant, yet all the strongest of the strangers could manage on a full day's hunt was two skinny birds. Hardly enough for one man, yet it would have to do for all six of them.

The warrior's thoughts were interrupted when the boy

sat up like a startled deer. As before, he looked directly at the warrior yet saw nothing. Then he headed back to join the others. Quietly the warrior worked his way around to the trees behind the fire.

SEVEN

Jack, Hudson, Staffe, Wydhowse, and Fanner were all gathered around the blaze. Moving aside, Jack beckoned me over to a space between him and his father.

"Come and sit with us, Al," he said as I approached. "Some of our bounty is almost ready and, as you can see, a few have not the patience to wait."

The two birds had been divided into six portions. Four were sizzling on sticks above the coals. The other two were being greedily devoured by Fanner and Wydhowse. The blood on their hands supported Jack's claim that their portions weren't cooked through yet. I sat beside Jack.

"We should complete our introductions," Jack said. "Myself and father you know. Philip Staffe is our carpenter and hunter." The big man nodded at me. "Syracke Fanner you also met. He has taken it upon himself to ensure we do not leave the Lord God Almighty out of our deliberations." Fanner ignored both Jack's comments and me. "Beside Syracke is Thomas Wydhowse, our mathematician and philosopher." Wydhowse nodded to me wearily and continued eating.

"This is what we are reduced to from the nine who began this adventure in the shallop some seven weeks ago. Adame Moore and Michael Butt were sorely ill and lasted but a few days. Like good sailors, we buried them at sea among the ice floes. Arnall Ludlowe fell into the depths of despair and passed to a better world these three weeks past. John King, the quartermaster, sometime mate, and the only man to raise arms to resist the mutineers, was the strongest among us. It was his work on the oars that mostly brought the shallop to this place. He died but two days past in a great fever and raving of his wife and children as if he were back in the bosom of his family. King and Ludlowe are buried yonder."

Jack waved his arm toward the two crude crosses. Then he lapsed into silence, his attention fixed on his portion of meat. The others also gazed hungrily at the meat over the fire.

Staffe spoke first. "I think the meat is done." He brought in his stick, and the others followed suit.

Jack had two sticks and handed one to me. "Here is your portion, Al."

"Why should he get a portion?" Fanner had finished his and was looking greedily at mine. "He is not one of us and we have greater need than this salvage."

"Our need may be the greater," Hudson replied, "but we must honour our guest as best we can, even in the poor circumstances we find ourselves."

"You will regret this unwarranted generosity, just as you now regret hoarding the cheeses on the ship." Angrily Fanner stood and limped to the hut. Hudson shook his head sadly.

"'Tis only that man's anger that keeps him alive to torment the rest of us," Staffe said between mouthfuls of meat.

I had been planning on offering my portion to be divided

among the others. Obviously I wasn't as hungry as they were and, to be honest, the grubby, half-cooked meat didn't look all that appetizing. After Fanner's outburst and Hudson's response, though, I felt obliged to eat as much as I could. I ate slowly and the others were finished long before me. Carefully they licked every drop of grease from their hands and dropped the cleaned bones into the pot. Then all eyes turned to watch me nibble on the still-bloody hunk in my hand. I felt uncomfortable.

"I think this will serve everyone better in the soup," I said, dropping my portion into the pot. An audible sigh escaped from the starving men as they relaxed a bit.

"So, young Master Al," Hudson addressed me, "tell us some tales of the land from which you come."

"As I said," I replied nervously, "my home is far away." How far, I hoped they would never guess, because then, apart from all the other complications of trying to explain my world to Henry Hudson, I would have to say I knew that none of my new companions would ever survive to see home again.

"My home is much different from this." I waved my arm to include the rough camp. "And I would happily tell you about it, but tell me," I said, attempting to change the subject, "how you came to be here."

"That is indeed a long and sad tale," Hudson began, "and the understanding of it is buried far in the past." He lapsed into silence.

Since no one else seemed eager to take up the tale, I decided to chance some flattery before he tried to ask me more awkward questions. "I would be interested to hear your tale My people tell many stories of you and your adventures, and I would have a lot of status if I could take home some that I heard directly from the great explorer himself." Out of the corner of my eye, I saw Jack smile.

My flattery seemed to rouse Hudson, and he looked up at

me. "You wish to hear my tale, do you? Well, perhaps it is time. I do feel the heavy burden of my years and oftimes I think I may not see my dear Katherine nor Oliver nor Richard again." At this point he looked over at Jack, who seemed about to interrupt, but his father hurried on, giving him no chance to contradict.

"My years began in 1570 when Good Queen Bess had but been on the throne a dozen years. Of my early life you need know little, save that it was passably comfortable and that my mind was continually engaged with the great voyages of that time. When I was eleven, I was blessed to meet the great Francis Drake after he returned from his voyage around the world. He suffered much, but returned rich with booty from the Spanish galleons who little suspected his presence off the coast of their American lands. He told great tales of wondrous places, but one stayed with me. He spoke of the Strait of Anian as if he had seen it with his own eyes. 'If we can navigate those waters,' he told me, 'we will have a Northwest Passage of great ease to take us to the wealth of Cathay. And it will be a route untroubled by the ships of the devilish Spanish king.' In my childish dreams I became the man who would chart that course and gain greatness for my country.

"My chance came more quickly than I could have hoped. In 1587 I was, through the offices of my father who realized by then that I was destined for a life on the sea, an able-bodied seaman with John Davis on his second great voyage to the north. I had been on short voyages around the coasts of England and knew the rudiments of sail and navigation.

"Of course, Davis was foiled by the ice, but I learned much of seamanship in the northern latitudes, reaching as we did the farthest point north ever reached to that date. I also saw the Furious Overfall, which all realized must come forth from some vast sea. Unfortunately the roaring of the waters and the rushing of the great blocks of ice forbade us passage, but both Davis and myself agreed that, could passage be made through the Furious Overfall, the route to Cathay would be most probable and the execution easy. That voyage and what we saw on it has been the guide to everything I have done since.

"The next year Davis sailed north again, but I was not with him, as Drake had need of every able-bodied seaman to withstand the Armada of the perfidious Spanish pretender." Hudson seemed to sit straighter and stronger as he recalled the battle. "I was on one of the ships that harried the Spaniards up the channel. We were smaller vessels but were more than their match in seamanship and gunnery. We were more manoeuvrable and could sail closer to the wind, so we harried them like terriers at a wounded deer. I was also there in the Calais Roads when the fire ships were sent in, flaming and blazing to spread panic among those overproud wooden citadels.

"The next day I was on the *Nonpareil* at Gravelines and sailed beneath the silent guns of the *San Martín*. She was little more than a hulk by then, her upper decks being a shambles and her hull wallowing low in the water. It was many nights later before I could sleep without the image of the blood of her brave sailors running out of the scuppers and haunting my dreams.

"After the Armada, there was no great interest in the northern lands, and I struggled to get commands where I could. Luckily I was not in London when the plague broke out in 1592. It was said that one in ten of the poor citizens were carried off and that the burial grounds were full to overflowing.

"In 1597 the Dutchman Willem Barents captured my imagination once more when his crew became the first to winter in the Arctic lands. Then my friend Richard Hakluyt published his famous tales of English seafarers. Davis was there as was the unlucky Martin Frobisher and the tragic Hugh Willoughby. I determined that one day my name would rank with theirs.

"But it was not until 1607 that I acquired my first command in the north, and it was to seek a Northeast Passage to Cathay around the shores of Muscovy. We sailed to the Spitzbergens and exceeded eighty degrees of latitude, but the ice and fog and storms forced our retreat. I was in favour of continuing by a Northwest Passage, but the crew was eager for home and they prevailed. We returned without gold and spices."

"But not empty-handed," Jack interrupted. "The reports of bays filled with whalefish and walruses have commenced a lucrative industry."

"Aye," Hudson replied with a smile, "but what are a few fish compared with the riches of the Orient? In any case, the following year the Muscovy Company again supplied the good ship *Hope-well*, and we once more set sail. On this occasion we kept close in by the shore of Norway, attempting to follow the inhospitable northern coast to the Orient. We reached as far as Nova Zembla where poor Barents had perished."

"And no wonder," Jack added. "It is a land so barren that no tree or plant can flourish. The world at the dawn of creation must have looked much like that."

"Indeed," Hudson agreed, "and the ice was again too heavy to allow us farther ventures. Having exhausted my requirement to the Muscovy Company, I once more headed for the northwest, but this time Juet spoke against me to the crew and they forced a return to London."

"Juet?" I said, biting my tongue in time to prevent my betraying the fact that I knew he had led the mutiny on the last voyage.

"Robert Juet," Hudson continued, "mate on three voyages

and my nemesis. A good sailor, but one cursed with an uncertain mind. He does not have the will to see the dangers through to success, yet he does have the speech to turn others against any project he does not find to his taste. I had hoped to improve him by example—he has the makings of a great sailor—but it was not to be."

"May he roast in hell for his treachery," Staffe growled vehemently.

"Well," Hudson said thoughtfully, "we shall all receive our just deserts come Judgement Day. But to continue my tale for our new friend. There was little interest in England in more voyages, but in Amsterdam I found the Dutchmen to be of a more adventurous cast. They fitted me with the *Half Moon*, the finest vessel I ever sailed in. They, too, wished for a Northeast Passage and commanded me accordingly. I knew there was no way through the masses of ice I had seen in previous years so, when we encountered ice north of Norway, I took it as an excuse and sailed west to Newfoundland and the Northwest Passage. I intended to make it through the Furious Overfall of Davis, but Juet talked against me to the crew and they refused. We went south to Manhattan Island from whence we discovered a great river that we sailed up a distance of some one hundred and fifty miles."

"Juet again took part against you, Father," Jack added. "You should have left him in the wilderness."

"Aye, perhaps, but would it have made me a better man to have done to him what he has done to me? In any case, he was not alone. The Dutchmen of the crew were unused to the cold climes and unwilling to continue. We returned to England where the authorities were most disconcerted that I had taken service with a foreign power. Nonetheless, a band of merchant adventurers took it upon themselves to finance yet one more try, and so, but a little over a year ago, we set sail from St.

Katherine's Pool. This time there was to be no doubt, and we sailed straight for the Furious Overfall and the many hardships that have brought us to this sorry pass."

Hudson paused and gazed thoughtfully into the fire. After a moment, he continued. "If only we had sailed to the west, we would be through the Strait of Anian and sampling the pleasures of Cathay by now."

"No!" I exclaimed without thinking. Hudson, Jack, and Staffe all looked up at me sharply.

"What say you?" Staffe asked. "Do you know the geography of this shore?"

I had to learn to control my tongue. I spoke slowly and carefully. "A little. My people in Ottawa have learned something through trade."

"Then speak!" Hudson interjected excitedly. "I would know where the strait lies."

"Not here," I said, shaking my head. "This is a huge bay. There is no outlet to the west."

Hudson stared at me intently. "The Strait of Anian lies to the north then?"

"Yes," I answered, "a long way to the north, and it's blocked by ice."

"I knew it!" Staffe shouted. "This is but a wild-goose chase. There is no way through to the Orient. We suffer for nought."

Hudson looked puzzled. "But Greene told me otherwise."

"What did he tell you?" I couldn't stop myself asking. Here might be the answer to one of the mysteries: why had Hudson secretly taken Greene with him?

Hudson turned his sunken gaze on me, but he was focusing on the far distance. "Knowing of my interest in the Strait of Anian, Greene came to my house after my return in the *Half Moon* and told me a tale. He said that a few years previous he had met an old sailor in a drinking house he was overly fond of frequenting. The man was far gone both in age and in his drink, but he told Greene a story. In his youth he had been a fisherman over on the Grand Banks of Newfoundland. One year, he could remember not exactly which but it was certainly while Good Queen Bess still reigned, he had rescued a dying man in an open boat."

The *Jonathan!* My mind leaped to the story my father had discovered, but I managed to keep silent as Hudson continued.

"He told the captain of his ship, the *Jonathan*, of a great sea he had visited and of the people who lived by its side and who looked like the natives of Cathay and used weapons much like those of Java and the islands around there. The man was much gone in sickness and starvation and died soon thereafter, but the captain brought his tale back and, I think, dined and drank more than once on the strength of its telling. At first I was not much inclined to place weight on Greene's telling, but he spoke well with a soft voice and he had a coin."

"A coin?" I asked, trying to hide my excitement.

"Aye," Hudson responded, digging deep into the leather pouch at his belt and withdrawing a gold coin. He passed it over to me.

There was no doubt. It was *the* gold coin I had found on the previous year's dig. It gleamed more brightly than when it had been rescued from the earth, but St. Michael, the dragon, and the ship were there just the same. My heart was racing, but I kept my voice calm. "What does this mean?"

"What indeed?" Hudson looked thoughtfully at the coin glinting in my hand. "Greene's story was that there were originally a pair of these the dead sailor had taken to the Great Sea. On the shores he had traded for skins with a local tribe of salvages. On departure he had given the chief of the salvages one of the coins as proof of his good intentions and so that future traders would know with whom they dealt.

"The dying man gave the coin to the captain, who never went to the Great Sea but kept the coin close to his heart. Greene claimed the captain gave it to him, although knowing more of the man now, I do wonder how he came to it. In any case, Greene used the coin to convince me of the veracity of his tale. He said he would give me the coin, which would surely help in our meetings with the salvages, on condition I take him with me on the voyage. Greene was no seaman, so I brought him aboard by subterfuge. How I regret that action now, but it is done."

Hudson lapsed into silence, and I handed the angel back to him. I could think of nothing to say. Greene, the trickster, had wormed his way aboard Hudson's ship with soft words. But were those words true? The angel was certainly real, as was the old document Dad had found, both of which appeared to support the story.

My thoughts were interrupted by a thin, reedy voice singing:

"Alas, my love, ye do me wrong
To cast me off discourteously;
And I have loved you so long,
Delighting in your company.

Greensleeves was all my joy,
Greensleeves was my delight;
Greensleeves was my heart of gold,
And who but Lady Greensleeves?"

We all listened as Wydhowse sang to himself, completely oblivious to the presence of the rest of us. The song was long, cataloguing all the things the singer had given Greensleeves to try to win her favour. It had all been in vain, and I wondered if Wydhowse was thinking of his family back in England as he sang it. Despite his weak voice, the words certainly seemed to strike a chord with the listeners, and no one interrupted him.

Eventually Wydhowse finished the song, and we sat in silence around the fire. Then Wydhowse spoke. There were tears in his eyes. "Master Staffe, would you be so kind as to help me to our house? I am greatly fatigued and would rest."

Staffe rose and almost carried Wydhowse to the shelter. Hudson, Jack, and I remained gazing at the dull coals.

Unseen, the warrior listened to the singing. It was not like his people's singing at all. It was quiet and monotonous—not a fitting song for a warrior. He doubted he would ever understand these strangers. His mind drifted back to the time the strangers had attempted to make contact with his people. It had been the spring, after the ice had melted enough to allow Hairy Face and some of his men to travel south in one of their smaller canoes. They had come ashore near the warrior's camp and gestured that they wanted to trade. Some of his people had panicked and run into the woods, but the others, led by the *okimah*, had set the woods on fire to keep the strangers away. Hairy Face had left.

On that occasion the temptation to make his presence known to the strangers had been almost overwhelming, but the warrior had obeyed the will of his band. The arrival of the strangers had been a signal of change. Nothing like this had ever happened before in the entire history of his people. He didn't know why, but he felt deeply that things could never be quite the same again. More of these strangers would come. If one canoe load came this far and suffered so much in a land they obviously did not know, they must be driven by such a strong curiosity that others would surely come. After these ones died, their companions would come looking for them. If some of these ones returned, then their stories would make others come to see for themselves.

Either way more of these strangers in their winged canoes would come to the warrior's land. Ignoring them would do no good. If these people were strong enough, they would take what they wanted, the warrior was sure of that. Better then to trade with them and become their friends. The *okimah* was wrong. There was going to be change and the people would have to realize that sooner or later. Maybe, by watching these people now, the warrior would learn enough to make the trading easier when it did eventually happen. Sighing, he watched as the singer was helped into the wooden teepee by the tall man.

EIGHT

Staffe returned to his seat by the fire. "I fear Wydhowse and Fanner are neither long for this world."

Hudson nodded, then turned to look at me. "How did you come to this place, Master Al?"

This was it. The direct question I had been dreading. Impossible-to-explain images of trains, pickup trucks, and helicopters flooded my tired brain.

"By canoe," I said, "but it hit a rock and was holed. I was attempting to walk back when I met Jack on the beach."

"Then it is possible to walk to this Ottawa of which you spoke?"

I was trapped. I couldn't mention the camp by the big rock without explaining why it wasn't there or, more correctly, wouldn't be there for centuries.

"Yes," I lied, "but it's very far. A canoe would be easier, but your boat's too big for the rivers that lead that way."

Hudson nodded. "And to what purpose came you here?"

That was a tough one. To dig up garbage tips to try to

prove someone came here before you didn't seem like a very good answer. "I came to see if the stories my people had heard of strangers visiting this land were true."

"The salvage who came to trade in the winter," Staffe interjected.

"It would seem so," Hudson said, "although we have probably been much observed without our knowing it. Certainly news travels fast in these lands. In any case, your arrival here, young Master Al, and your knowledge of this land I take as a sign. We must look to our own resources if we are to escape. Thus we must make contact with the French at Quebec." Hudson's eyes met mine, and there was an intensity to them that seemed to burn out of the sunken cheeks. "Will you help us to that end, or at least to achieve your Ottawa?"

There was no way I could refuse the plea. In any case, what would be the point? I had nowhere else to go. I had no control over returning to my own time and, if I was stuck here in 1611, I was in the same predicament as Hudson and his party.

"Certainly," I replied. "My people would be honoured to meet you." At least my father would.

"Good." Hudson gave me a weak smile. "Then there is no point in delay. Come the morrow, you Jack, Philip, and Al must go south. You will—"

"What of you, Father?" Jack interrupted.

"I will remain here with Wydhowse and Fanner. I am too old and weary for the journey you have before you. God willing, you will return with succour before the winter sets in."

It was a slim hope—we could all see that—but what choice was there? Wydhowse and Fanner could barely walk a few hundred metres, let alone the hundreds of kilometres of hard going before we could hope for assistance, and Hudson wasn't in much better shape. Jack, Staffe, and I were easily the fittest. But even we had no chance that I could see to negotiate successfully what must be close to a thousand kilometres between James Bay and Quebec. Our only chance was to meet up with some friendly First Nations people.

Hudson must have been thinking much the same. Reaching back into his pouch, he took out the angel.

"Jack, take this. If there be any truth in Greene's tale, then there are, somewhere upon these shores, people who may yet recognize this coin and for its sake offer shelter and succour to the bearer."

Jack took the coin from his father's hand and looked at it. The firelight glistened on the tears in his eyes. He opened his mouth to speak, but Hudson didn't give him the chance.

"And there is one more thing you must take," he said, reaching beneath the folds of his coat and producing a small leather-bound book. "This is my journal. It tells of all our trials and how we have come to this sorry pass. I think Juet, Greene, and the others will either starve or drown long 'ere they spy England. If any are to know of our exploits and our great discoveries, it will be from our mouths or through the pages of this writing. Keep it secure and pass it on to safe hands."

"I will, Father." Tears ran freely down Jack's cheeks. "But is there no other way?"

"None," his father replied, "and even this is by no means certain. We must all do what we can. I take comfort from the arrival of Master Al and his strange knowledge of our doings. I think it will be through him that our story will be told."

Hudson turned his gaze back from Jack to me. There was a pleading look in his eyes. I felt responsibility weigh heavily on me. How could I have an effect on what happened here? These events had all run their course centuries before I was even born. Nevertheless, I nodded. "I will do my best to help." This seemed to satisfy him.

"And now, with some food in my belly, I would sleep," the explorer said, standing. "Tomorrow will bring what it must."

"Aye." Staffe rose beside his captain. "It will that and I think I, too, will have need of what hours of rest I can obtain tonight. I bid you a good sleep."

With that Hudson and Staffe retreated to the hut. On the way Staffe paused to build up the small secondary fire in the doorway, placing a green branch on top of it. Thick smoke billowed. "That might discourage some of the damnable insects of these parts," he said, ducking from sight.

For a long time Jack and I gazed into the embers of the dying fire. My thoughts were confused. I felt myself drawn into these events almost against my will. It was easier to accept that tomorrow I would set off with Jack and Staffe to seek help for an abandoned Henry Hudson than it was to try to find an explanation for my situation. If there was an explanation, I was coming to think that it involved insanity, and I didn't want to think too hard about that.

Eventually Jack broke the silence. "Well, Al, what do you make of all this?"

"I don't know," I answered honestly. "But I think your father's right. We must try to get help."

"Aye," he said quietly, "and I think he puts much hope in you. Is it a long and arduous journey to Ottawa?"

"Yes," I replied, "but, as your father said, there is no choice. Jack," I continued, asking a question that had been on my mind since I had first realized who I was speaking to, "what happened on the ship? Why did Greene and Juet lead a mutiny against your father?"

"Because they are rogues, thieves, and scoundrels," Jack said. Then, in a quieter voice, he added, "But that is not all. Not every one of the mutineers is such. Some are good men. Robert Bylot for one. He is a fine navigator and a man who will go far in exploration if he so chooses—and if he survives. Abacuck Prickett for another. He kept a journal of our voyage, which I pray may survive. And if I look to honesty, my father was not without blame.

"He is a great man, but he has a headstrong spirit. The Northwest Passage has been an obsession with him as long as I have lived, and Greene's story merely fuelled his passion. To be the discoverer of the route to Cathay, he pushed his crews farther than men were like to go.

"We suffered much last winter. The hunting was poor and we could find no salvages to trade with. When the ice freed the *Discovery*, we were in sore straits, near to starvation and sick from scurvy. We had but food for fourteen days more. Everyone—I admit myself, too—was desperate to make the greatest speed home. But Father delayed. He had made great and wondrous discoveries, but he had not reached the shores of Cathay and was loath to return without a hold full of spices and gold. He also felt assured that we were so close to the Orient that we would obtain succour the more quickly by sailing west to the islands of the emperor of Japan."

Jack fell silent, and I didn't want to disturb him. After a few minutes, he looked at me. "Al, you are a Christian, although of a strange sort. Do your people live their lives as Christians?"

"They try to," I replied, wondering where the conversation was going.

"My father does, too," Jack went on, "at least as far as he is able. He would rather turn the other cheek and reach an agreement by compromise than fight with sword and club and impose his will. Some take that as a sign of weakness, and perhaps it is on a ship in a desperate situation in the wilderness.

"He played favourites, giving to Greene a coat that by the traditions of the sea should have been auctioned to the crew.

He threatened men with punishment and then was loath to carry the punishment out. He asked advice in the belief that all on such a perilous undertaking should have a say, yet it was looked upon by some as a weakness in one who should be commanding firmly.

"This last spring, when the ice released us, we were most in need of strong leadership. Father tried to provide it, but he was much broken in spirit and kept his counsel to himself, not even sharing it with me. There was a feeling among some that, if our lives were to be saved, others would have to take direction of the ship.

"Father distributed all the cheese that remained and counselled the men to save their portions, but some, Greene included, ate all theirs immediately, leaving nothing aside for the morrow. Then Greene began putting about tales of hoarded food and saying that only some could be saved and that others must be cast adrift. I think not many fully believed him, but in desperation and with Greene's and Juet's threats, there was not much sick men could do."

Jack's eyes took on a faraway look as he gazed out into the darkness, remembering. "It was a Sunday morning, the twenty-second day of June. My bunk was outside the galley, between the two Wilsons, Edward the surgeon and William the boatswain. The latter was heavily in with the mutineers, and I had noted that he had not come to his bunk the night before. I awoke once to the sound of his voice issuing from the neighbouring gun room and being quickly silenced by Juet, who kept quarters there. I thought nothing at the time. Perhaps if I had...

"The first I knew was awaking with Wilson's hand over my mouth and his voice in my ear: 'Stay silent, young Master Hudson, and no harm will attend thee.' Drowsed by sleep, I obeyed and followed the man forward. The first I knew of treachery was coming on deck to see Father with his hands bound behind his back. Shaking free of Wilson, I ran to Father and asked what was going on. He said to be of stout heart, that there were those who thought to run the ship better than her rightful masters, but that they had promised no harm should befall us.

"Just then there was a commotion from the hold and Juet's voice screaming for aid and saying that he was being attacked by King and like to be killed. Thomas and Wilson ran to assist, and King was brought up, much bloodied but still defiant. 'Ye shall all hang,' he said.

"Greene answered that he would rather hang at home than starve in the wilderness. Then we and those too sick to resist were bundled into the shallop and lowered over the side. Prickett spoke up for us but was silenced by threats from Greene, and Staffe alone voluntarily joined his master.

"We were all allowed to take only a few clothes except Staffe, who took his chest, a pot, and his matchlock fowling piece. And grateful have we been for even those meagre wares, for without them how would we have caught or cooked even the poor game we have found?

"We raised the sail on the shallop and near caught the *Discovery* so intent were the devils on plundering our goods, but they spotted us, raised their sail, and swept from view. Some were of the view that we should follow and attempt our own way back to England, but in our sickened condition it was a false hope. Thus we came to this place, and your arrival proves we decided right."

I felt suddenly very worn by the weight of having these men's hopes resting on my shoulders. "I'll do my best," I said weakly.

Jack smiled. "That is all any can do. But I think Master Staffe was correct and we will be needing what rest we can achieve tonight. My task is to sleep by the fire and keep it built through the night. If the rain holds off, it is not too bad. Will you join me?"

"Yes," I said.

With that Jack built up the fire to a sizable blaze, and we settled down as comfortably as possible within the circle of its warmth. Only then did I realize how tired I was. My last thought before I slept was a question—what year would it be when I awoke?

From the darkness the warrior watched the two boys settle down. The light of the fire did not extend far, and he had been concealed close enough to hear clearly every word of the talk. It had meant nothing to him, but something he had seen had sent a quiver of recognition through him.

At one point Hairy Face had given a glinting circle to one of the boys. It had caught the firelight like the reddish metal that sometimes came from the north, but it reminded the warrior of something else. The *okimah* had one the same. It had been given to the previous *okimah* who had died ten winters ago. He had told a tale of getting it from a band of *Omashkekowak*— Swampy Cree—that he had found dying in their village of a strange sickness. The old *okimah* had not wanted to approach too closely, but one of the sick men had called to him and thrown the bright circle to him.

The dying warrior had said the circle was a powerful gift from gods who had visited in a flying ship. He said whoever kept the circle would be visited again by the gods, who had many wonders and who would make themselves known by showing the people another circle the same as the one he threw. The sick man said his people must have offended the gods since they were now all dying of this strange sickness, but that the *okimah* should keep the circle safe against the gods' return. Now the gods were back.

The warrior did not believe these strangers were gods. Gods would not starve in a land of plenty. They were men like him. Men with strange habits and many wondrous things, but men just the same.

The warrior knew what he must do. This news would change the *okimah*'s mind. Now he would have to trade with these people. Tomorrow the warrior would start back for his village to give this startling news. Tonight he would bed down nearby. Silently the warrior turned and worked his way into the deeper darkness. He was so intent on his progress that he did not notice the dark figures threading through the trees.

NINE

I awoke just as dawn was beginning to lighten the eastern sky. I had slept surprisingly long and deeply and felt rested and comfortable—at least until I opened my eyes. There was the hut, with the small fire in front of it, and Jack's shadowy form bending over the main fire, which was reduced to glowing embers. I was still out of my own time. Somehow having spent a night here made the whole experience more real—and more serious. It seemed less likely that it was a hallucination and, if it wasn't that, what was it? How long would I be here? How much time was passing in my world? What was Dad doing?

My questions were interrupted by the appearance of Wydhowse from the hut. He didn't look as if a night's sleep had refreshed him at all. With barely a look around, he dragged his hunched form toward the trees and prepared to relieve himself. I supposed that if there was nothing I could do about where and when I was, I should at least get up and help Jack with the fire.

A low hiss and a soft thunk were all I heard. Wydhowse

straightened and took a step backward. The sounds were repeated. This time Wydhowse staggered visibly. Slowly he turned. He had a puzzled expression on his face as he looked down. Obviously he couldn't understand what two long, thin, feathered shafts were doing sticking out of his chest. Ineffectually he pawed at the arrows. Then, with a surprised gasp, he collapsed in a heap.

I was on my feet before Wydhowse's body hit the ground. Jack didn't seem to notice that anything was wrong.

"Jack!" I screamed. "We're being attacked."

He looked up at me. As he did so, an arrow clanged off the rock at his feet. Another hissed uncomfortable close to my right ear. Leaping over the fire, I grabbed Jack's sleeve and ran toward the hut. Staffe appeared in the doorway.

"Get in!" I yelled at him. He stepped aside just as Jack and I bundled into the dark interior, scattering the remains of the small fire. We were accompanied by an arrow that embedded itself in the flimsy wall, its wickedly pointed stone tip protruding a full twenty centimetres inside.

"What...?" Hudson began.

"We're being attacked," I said. "Wydhowse is dead."

An arrow found a gap in the wall, flew in, and fell to the floor beside Jack. Automatically he picked it up. Another buried itself in a branch, making the whole wall shake. Jack and I huddled on the floor, while Hudson looked about in confusion. Fanner crouched in a corner, his lips moving frantically in what sounded like a prayer. Only Staffe's activity was focused. He had his ancient musket across his knees and was concentrating on the complex mechanism above the trigger.

"Why doesn't he fire it?" I asked.

"He must light the match first," Jack answered.

I didn't understand, but I didn't want an explanation right now. Crawling to one side, I peered between a couple of branches. It wasn't an encouraging view. I counted six figures advancing from the trees. They were crouched over and moving slowly. Their bodies were almost naked, covered only by rough leggings and breastplates of wooden slats. Their heads were shaved, leaving topknots that were tied behind and from which assorted feathers dangled. Every exposed centimetre of skin was painted, usually black or red. Four of the warriors carried bows with arrows strung in them. The others held wicked-looking, curved clubs. Even moving slowly, they would be here soon. As I watched, one of the warriors drew his bow and loosed an arrow at the hut, where it lodged in a branch.

"Hurry!" I said urgently. Staffe ignored me. He had an ember from the small fire and was blowing on it. A thick taper was attached to the top of his gun, and I assumed this was what had to be lit before the contraption would fire. It would take too long. A bizarre thought crossed my overstressed mind. What if I died here and my father dug up my bones four hundred years in the future? It didn't bear thinking about. Fortunately I was interrupted by Fanner.

"Seek ye the Lord and he shall take ye unto his bosom!" he shouted. I turned to see him standing beside Jack, although he was hunched by the low roof. Jack was looking up at him, still holding the shaft of the arrow in his hand. For some reason he had broken the stone tip off.

"Sit, Fanner," Hudson commanded, reaching out to grab the man.

Fanner brushed his hand aside and headed for the door. "Save ye the heathen in the wilderness," he shouted, stepping outside.

"Come back, you fool!" Hudson cried, but Fanner ignored him.

I returned my attention to the hole in the wall. At Fanner's appearance the warriors stopped. Fanner was now shouting biblical phrases at them. The men looked uncertainly at one another. Slowly they began to retreat. I held my breath. Perhaps they had a taboo against killing someone as obviously crazy as Fanner. They were certainly unsure what to do. As Fanner raved, they moved backward, bows and clubs held low.

"I am the mouthpiece of the Lord God of Hosts," Fanner shouted, throwing his arms wide. "List unto me and ye shall be saved. Ignore the Word and ye shall be smitten just as Joshua smote the walls of Jericho."

One of the warriors stopped retreating. He was the tallest and carried a long club with a knot of wood on the end into which a piece of sharp rock was embedded. His face was divided by a horizontal line of paint. It ran across his cheeks, just under his eyes. Below the line was midnight-black; above it was blood-red. He began shouting at his companions, his teeth startlingly white against the paint. The other warriors hesitated but made no move. With a yell the tall warrior leaped forward and faced Fanner. The two men stood, their faces mere centimetres apart, each screaming unintelligibly at the other.

What occurred next happened so fast that it was difficult to distinguish individual elements from the blur of motion. The warrior let out an unearthly shriek and jumped a full half metre into the air. As he did, he raised his club and brought it crashing down on the top of Fanner's head. Instantly the biblical torrent ceased. Fanner's body collapsed onto the ground as if his bones had suddenly turned to water. With a second shout the warrior was on top of Fanner's prone body, kneeling across his shoulders. Dropping his club, he reached around his belt and extracted what looked like a long, sharp piece of black rock. Grabbing the limp Fanner's hair in his left hand, he began working with long, sweeping strokes. In an instant he was back on his feet, waving a lock of blood-caked hair around his head. He shook his grisly trophy at his companions, yelling and pointing at the hut. Given new courage by their companion's violence, the other five warriors rejoined the attack.

In shock I watched the band approach. The air was filled with bloodcurdling cries and the sound of arrows thudding into the wall of our fragile fortress. I was terrified. A horrible death was only metres away from me, and yet I was too scared even to run away. Not that I could see that doing much good. These men knew these woods. Even in the unlikely event that I got to the trees alive, they would probably only regard it as sport to hunt me down at their leisure. What could I do?

My question was answered by a thunderous roar from beside my left ear. The tall warrior, who was now only about five metres from me, was violently thrown backward and crashed to the ground. His companions stopped and gazed in shock at his motionless body. Then, as the smoke from Staffe's musket wafted across my view, they turned and ran into the trees.

With my ears ringing from the musket's report, I turned back to the scene in the hut. Staffe was already busily beginning the complex process of reloading his weapon. Jack, like me, was standing by the wall where he had been watching the drama unfold, and Hudson was crouched in the centre of the floor. Crude sleeping mats, rough blankets of hide, and a few pitiful personal possessions littered the ground. Against the opposite wall stood a dark wooden chest, and beside it was a wooden spear. Hudson broke the silence. "Why did they attack us? We mean them no harm."

"What man can say why salvages do anything?" Staffe replied, "But attack us they certainly did and, as poor Fanner proved, the Lord will not help us. It is up to us to help ourselves."

"You think they will attack again?" Jack's voice was worried.

"Aye," Staffe said, standing. "Once they recover from their shock, they will return, and I doubt if my musket will send them running next time."

"Then you must leave with all haste." Hudson rose to his feet as he spoke. "While the salvages are yet in confusion, you may find a way unnoticed into the woods. Philip, leave me your musket, which in any case I think will be of little use in the forests, and with that and my knife I shall attempt to delay them while you make good your escape."

"No!" Jack's shout echoed in my still-ringing ears. "I will not leave you, Father. Either you will come or I will stay, but we shall not be separated."

Hudson took a step toward Jack. "Your loyalty to me I have never doubted," he said, putting an arm around his son. "And as you well know, I have never forced upon you a course of action you did not wish. But in this I must be obeyed. I cannot walk the many miles it must be to our young friend's home. You cannot carry me. The only result of my attendance with you would be to slow all down. In that case, either these salvages would overtake us within but a few hours or, if we by some miracle avoided them, we would be doomed to a slow and painful starvation in the wilderness. Here, I can at least give you a chance. We must not all pass away without our story being told. That must be your goal, Jack, and my staying can help you toward it."

Jack clutched his father, sobs wracking his body.

"Your mother said I should not bring you on this voyage," Hudson continued. "She had a premonition that I put down to mere vapours. But I see now she was right and I should have attended her words with more care. I shall make amends the only way I can, by giving you a chance to return to her. Am I not right, Philip?"

"You are," Staffe replied quietly. "There is no other way, Jack. The world must know of your father's greatness, and you must be the one to tell of it. But we must not delay. Each moment the salvages recover some of their courage."

"Aye, you must go." Hudson pulled away from his son. "Come, Jack, help me to break a hole in the back wall farthest from our enemies." With his arm still around Jack, Hudson moved across the littered floor, and the pair began picking at the loose branches of the wall.

"Here, young Al," Staffe said, handing me a knife. "We cannot take much on our travels, but this will be of use."

I took the knife and slid it into my belt as Staffe grabbed an axe from the wooden chest. He also took a curved gunpowder horn with a metal lid, a small grey flint for fire-starting, a ball of twine, and some needles. He placed them in a crude leather bag that he swung over his shoulder. Hudson and Jack had by this time made a hole large enough for a man to crawl through. I looked back through the opposite wall. The bodies of Fanner, Wydhowse, and the tall warrior still lay in the open. There was no sign of movement from the trees.

"Each take a single blanket," Staffe said, still organizing. "Now we must go."

I grabbed a hide blanket and folded it roughly into a sleeping roll. Staffe did the same. Jack was slower, his face heavily stained with tears.

"Here," I said, picking up a second blanket. "I'll take yours."

Jack smiled weakly.

"You must no longer delay," Hudson said urgently. "Go deep in the woods. If in truth the salvages have vanished, I shall wait until I am sure and endeavour to join you there. Now make haste."

"Farewell, Henry Hudson," Staffe said. "It has been an

honour to be under your command, even though matters have not worked out as we would have wished." With that, Staffe shook Hudson's hand and ducked through the hole in the wall.

Hudson embraced his son, who was crying again. "Go now, Jack, and may God be with you."

Jack didn't want to let his father go. Putting my arm around his shoulder, I eased him toward the hole. "Come on, Jack, we've got to go now," I said as gently as I could. As I moved past Hudson, I looked up at him. There were tears in his eyes, but he still managed a thin smile. I nodded in what I hoped was a reassuring and adult way. As a last thought, I grabbed the spear from the wall and ducked out the hole.

Outside it was fearfully bright after the dark interior. The trees were only about fifteen metres away. Our route would be hidden by the hut, unless our attackers had circled around. Crouching low, Staffe led the way in an awkward run. Feeling overloaded with the two blankets under my arm, the spear in my hand, and trying to encourage Jack along, I followed.

The trip was slow, but it wasn't interrupted by an angry shout or the hiss of an arrow. The dark of the trees offered welcoming shelter. Without hesitating, Staffe pressed on deeper into the shadows.

We travelled in silence for a long time. Jack was barely aware of his surroundings, and I frequently had to prevent him from stumbling into tree trunks. He was sobbing quietly. I felt like crying, too. How would I feel leaving my father behind to certain death? It didn't bear thinking about. Dad and I didn't get along sometimes, but he was always there for me in his own way. A wave of sadness swept over me as I thought of my situation. Maybe he wasn't there for me anymore! Maybe both Jack and I had lost our fathers. With an effort I pushed the thought from my mind, steadied Jack, and carried on.

After what I thought must have been about an hour of slow progress over deadfall, swampy ground, and occasionally thick underbrush, we reached a small clearing by a sizable stream. Given the direction I thought we had been travelling, this must be the stream that ran out beside Hudson's camp. Exhausted, we lay on the bank and drank the cold, clear water.

Staffe finished first and sat up. "I think we have put some distance between ourselves and the salvages. We will wait here a while and recover our strength. Master Al, in which direction must we set off to reach your home with the most expedience?"

"Well..." I began hesitantly, unsure what to answer to the impossible question. "I think—"

I was interrupted by a low, distant thud. Jack was on his feet in an instant. Staffe looked away from me and back the way we had come. For a moment I was confused. Then it dawned on me. What we had heard was the report of a musket, and there was no denying what it meant. Jack sank to the ground, his body ravaged by renewed sobs. There could be no doubt he was on his own now. I felt tears welling in my eyes. Was I alone, too?

The warrior had been travelling for some time when he heard the dull noise of the stranger's weapon. It pleased him. Perhaps they had managed to bring down a deer. If so, it would have been mostly a matter of luck, but the meat would help them while he was away. He hurried on through the trees and was too far distant to hear the second musket shot a little time later.

The sun was directly over his head when the warrior met the war party. As he crossed a small clearing, it materialized from the trees around him: twenty men, heavily armed with bows and clubs and dressed and painted for war. The warrior had a moment of trepidation and even half reached for the knife on his belt before he recognized the others. They were from his band and they were led by the *okimah*.

After the usual greetings, the *okimah* explained what had happened in the warrior's absence. Apparently a hunter had spotted a party of *Iri-akhoiw* travelling toward the shore of the Great Water. They were obviously in the people's lands for one reason only—to capture slaves to take home. To achieve this they would murder and plunder at will and cause much weeping among the people.

Since there were only a few places on the Great Water shore where such a large party of *Iri-akhoiw* could camp, they should not be hard to find, and the *okimah* had decided to launch a surprise attack first, kill as many of the invaders as possible, and drive the rest away.

The warrior instantly forgot about the bright circle and the tale he was going to tell the *okimah*. That could wait. The threat to his land and people from the *Iri-akhoiw* was more immediate. Exchanging words of greeting with his friends, the warrior joined the raiding party as they resumed their journey to the Great Water. He was completely focused on his new task, except for a tiny worm of doubt working at the back of his mind. Perhaps the weapon report he had heard that morning had not signalled a successful hunt. Perhaps there was a more sinister motivation.

TEN

By an unspoken agreement, we ignored the implications of the second musket shot, at least to one another. In our own minds I think we all knew what it meant. Jack sat in miserable silence while Staffe and I tied the blankets into rolls that could be slung across our backs. This would help free our hands and make the going easier.

"So, Master Al," Staffe said when we were finished our preparations, "in which way must we go?"

As I worked, I had been thinking. I knew from my father's maps that the Nottaway River ran into the southern end of James Bay and had been used by First Nations people as part of their trading circle between where we were and the St. Lawrence Valley. I also knew that the Nottaway rose in some lakes inland, but my geography was hazy after that. At least travelling up the river we would be going in the right direction. I didn't think there was much chance that we'd reach Ottawa or Montreal—in fact, I was sure my two companions never would—but we had to do something, if only to avoid falling into depression.

My plan also had the advantage of allowing us to travel along the shoreline of James Bay, at least to begin with, and that would be easier than clambering through the woods. And the faster we travelled, the faster we'd put distance between ourselves and our attackers. It would also mean passing by the site of Dad's camp. I knew there would be nothing there, but I still had a strong desire to visit the site. Perhaps, in the back of my mind, I hoped that visiting a place I was going to be in the future might trigger travel back to my own time.

"There's a river to the south," I told Staffe. "We're probably far enough inland now. If we curve back around to the coast, the going will be much easier."

I was surprised at how confident I sounded. I wasn't used to taking charge. Staffe nodded and, picking up our blankets, we splashed across the stream and continued through the trees.

The going was no easier, and we had an unpleasant hour squelching through a large patch of muskeg, but by midday we reached the coast. Despite the weakened condition of my companions and the fact that we had only eaten a few handfuls of blackberries all day, our rate of travel increased dramatically.

As we progressed, I began to relax. I was tired, hungry, and wet, but the sun was shining, so I wasn't too cold and sometimes my footwear almost dried out. Mostly, though, I was simply relieved there was now a good distance between ourselves and the horrors of the dawn attack. I couldn't rid myself of two vivid images from the morning: the picture of the tall warrior standing astride poor Fanner's body, waving his bloody trophy and screaming in exultation; and the look of sadness in Hudson's eyes as I left him to his fate.

I think we were in mild shock after the morning attack. All we could do was plod along as the surrounding world of water, trees, and screaming seabirds blurred to a haze. The only thing that roused me was the familiar feeling I was being watched from the trees. I looked up several times but only saw dark shadows.

At one point I became aware that Jack was singing:

"Sweet smelling beds of lilies and of roses
Which rosemary banks and lavender encloses.
There grows the gillyflower, the mint, the daisy
Both red and white, the blue-veined violet,
The purple hyacinth, the spike to please thee,
The scarlet-dyed carnation bleeding yet."

On noticing my presence at his side, he looked up. His eyes were red from crying. "For all the time he spent in forbidding places, my father was fond of a peaceful garden filled with the colours and perfumes of plants. He loved the verse of Humphrey Gifford and agreed with him that plants should be grown for their colour, scent, and shape as much as for their medicinal and food value. Of course, many can be grown for both as my father did in the garden of our house in London. He often said that when he returned from Cathay, he would bring with him many strange plants to ornament his garden and please him in his old age."

"Perhaps he will," I said, not believing it but feeling I had to say something positive. "Perhaps the musket shot we heard—"

"No!" Jack's shout was unexpectedly violent. "He will not sit in his garden. He will not see the shores of Cathay. He is gone to another world, if not better than this, then at least free of its cares. I think before we reach this Ottawa of yours, we may all envy him his journey."

I fell silent. There was obviously nothing I could say to comfort Jack. We trudged on.

As the sun descended toward the horizon, Staffe called a

halt. "We must rest. Perhaps we might find some berries or be blessed with a bird for our sustenance. In any case, we must rest. How far is it to this river, young Al?"

"A long way yet," I answered, though I really had little idea.

Staffe nodded thoughtfully. "Well," he said eventually, taking his flint from his leather pouch, "let us sit here a while. Jack, if you and Al would go into the woods, perhaps you might find some berries to assuage our hunger. I shall gather wood and commence a fire. It will cheer us and we are far enough from the salvages that we need not fear the smoke."

Nodding in agreement, Jack and I threw down our blankets and moved toward the trees. I took the spear I had been carrying, just in case we came upon something edible.

The trees were widely spaced here and the ground was dry. There were several open areas covered with a carpet of brown pine needles and numerous low bushes with broad, waxy leaves. The bushes carried crops of dark blue berries. Hesitantly I tried one. It was bitter but not unpleasant. With the taste of the juice in my mouth, my hunger overcame me. Laying down the spear, I began picking berries for all I was worth and stuffing them into my mouth. I could feel the juice trickling down my chin, but I didn't even pause to wipe it away.

So intent was I on my feast that I wasn't even aware of my attacker until it was too late. The first thing I knew was when a pair of strong hands grabbed me from behind and pinned my arms to my sides. I struggled, kicking and throwing my head back in an attempt to hit my assailant, but nothing worked. I was powerless in the strong grip. All I could do was warn my companions. I opened my mouth to shout, but before a sound came out a sharp pain exploded at the back of my head and blackness swept over me.

I came to back on the beach with a serious headache. I was lying on my left side on the sharp rocks of the shore. My hands were firmly tied behind me. Tilting my head back, I could see Jack crumpled in a heap near my feet. He wasn't moving, but the fact that his hands were also tied encouraged me to think he wasn't dead. I couldn't say the same for Staffe. The lower half of his body was draped over a log, one arm leaning against it and pointing grotesquely into the air. Fortunately I couldn't see his head, but the handle of his axe protruded over the log and told me the story. In front of him were the pitiful beginnings of the fire he had been working on when he was attacked. Behind him stood four of the painted warriors who had attacked us that morning and who we had foolishly thought we were well clear of. They were talking animatedly. With horror I noticed that one of them had a lock of familiar grey hair tied to his belt.

As if he had felt my gaze, the warrior with the hair at his belt suddenly glanced in my direction. Seeing me looking at him, he gave a fierce shout, leaped over Staffe's body, and stood above me. I felt my hair grabbed painfully and my head and shoulders pulled off the ground. Out of the corner of my eye I saw sunlight glint off a knife blade I recognized as Henry Hudson's. I closed my eyes and waited for the blow.

Nothing happened. Cautiously opening my eyes, I noticed a fifth warrior. He was standing in front of me, firmly grasping the wrist of my attacker in his right hand. His left hand and arm hung uselessly by his side, caked from the shoulder down in dried blood. He spoke urgently to his companion, who eventually relaxed and replaced Hudson's knife in his belt. Turning away, he aimed a kick at the prone Jack who, I was relieved to hear, let out a low grunt of protest. Stepping over the log, the warrior bent to retrieve the axe that protruded from Staffe's body. Fortunately the log obscured my view of the grisly task.

From what I had seen I could work out something of what

must have happened that morning. Once they had overcome the shock of Staffe's musket felling their leader, they had attacked once more. Perhaps they had spread around the hut this time. In any case, Hudson had managed a shot at one of them, wounding him in the shoulder. After that it would have been over quickly. I assumed the one with the grey hair at his belt had been the one to finish Jack's father.

What amazed me was the speed with which the five men, even when one was seriously wounded, had travelled down the coast to catch us. They had probably been watching us for some time. Seeing us split up, they had taken their chance. Staffe was obviously the strongest of us and hence the greatest threat to them. He probably never even saw them coming. With Staffe dead it was an easy matter to capture Jack and me.

But what were their intentions? They weren't going to kill us out of hand. The fact that I was lying here thinking about it proved that. But what did they want us for? Who were they? From their shaved heads and topknots I got a vague memory of pictures of Iroquois and Huron warriors, but didn't they live way south of here, along the St. Lawrence River and down into New York State? What were they doing up here by James Bay?

Then a chilling memory came back to me. Part of the trading network my father was studying involved slaves. Bands from the south sometimes headed north on raids to capture slaves for their villages. The little I could remember was that the slaves were well treated and adopted as family members once they had been accepted. What caused the chills was the recollection that they were often tortured brutally to see if they were brave enough to be accepted. I doubted very much if I was.

My unpleasant thoughts were interrupted by the approach of two of the warriors. Grabbing me roughly under the arms, they hauled me to my feet where I swayed unsteadily, trying to keep my gaze away from the top half of Staffe's body, which I could now see over the log.

Jack, too, was hauled up, and I was glad to see he was awake and could stand, even if unsteadily. I doubted if our captors would waste much time carrying an unconscious prisoner.

The wounded warrior set off along the beach, his useless arm dangling absurdly by his side. The others clustered around us, herding us forward with kicks and painful prods from their axes. It was difficult going, and I wasn't keen to arrive wherever it was we were being taken.

The warrior crouched in the dense bush, watching the stockade. It was roughly made but strong enough to prevent a surprise attack. This was a large raiding party. The warrior felt no fear, but he did feel unlucky that these barbarous *Iri-akhoiw* had chosen now, just when he had found a way to persuade the *okimah* to trade with the strangers, to invade his lands. The *Iri-akhoiw* did not come up this far often, being tied as they were to the ground where they scraped a pitiful existence. But then this was the great trading circle. It brought useful stone for spear and arrow points to his people, but it also occasionally brought raiding parties, such as the ones who had built this stockade on his shore.

The warrior viewed the *Iri-akhoiw* with scorn. His life was honourable, moving with the cycles of the animals and seasons and taking what he needed from the wealth of the land about him. It was obvious to him that the spirits of the world wanted the people to take what they needed as long as they did it with proper ritual and respect. Did not the spirits provide the abundant caribou, beaver, and geese; the sparkling lakes rich with fish; the deep, whispering forest crowded with berries? There was no need to steal people from far away. If the corn growers from the long houses to the south needed to do that it simply showed their weakness, and the warrior and his colleagues would make them pay for trying.

The war party had found the *Iri-akhoiw* camp where they had thought it would be, but it was well established on a wide clearing by the shore and difficult to attack. The *Iri-akhoiw* had chosen their campsite well. The stockade was strong and built against a large rock. The entrance faced the open area so that attackers would have to run over much unprotected ground before they came to blows. The warrior could see no way in.

The war party had withdrawn to a safer distance, leaving the warrior to watch and wait. They would return after dark to see what he had discovered. The warrior had been watching for several hours now and the sun was already touching the horizon. Small parties of *Iri-akhoiw* had been out hunting or collecting shellfish, but they had returned. A large fire was being built within the stockade, and through the gaps in the wall of branches, the warrior could make out moving figures.

The warrior's concentration was disturbed by a noise from along the beach. Another hunting party was returning. As they moved into his field of vision, the warrior almost gasped. The party was led by a wounded warrior and had captured two prisoners—the two boys from Hairy Face's camp. Had that been the meaning of the loud noise he had heard in the morning?

As the warrior watched, the *Iri-akhoiw* leader shouted. Others came out of the stockade to welcome him, and his companions prodded the boys viciously to hurry them up. Amid much shouting, the new arrivals were ushered into the stockade and the gate was closed.

The warrior felt sad. He knew the others must be dead, so there was now no chance of contacting them and trading. He also knew the two boys soon would be dead and that the manner of their dying would not be pleasant.

ELEVEN

The huge fire cast its glow over everything within the stockade. Almost naked dancers, their bodies glistening with sweat, gyrated around the fire. Shadows flickering wildly over the stockade walls, the huts, and the rock against which Jack and I sat.

It was my rock. This was my father's camp, but much different from when I had last seen it.

The last hour of daylight had been a nightmare of exhausted stumbling down the beach. Jack and I had been forced almost to run to keep up with our captors. If we slowed or fell down, which we did often and painfully since our hands were still tied behind us, we were beaten until we continued. My body was covered with cuts and bruises that ached dreadfully. It had been almost a relief to arrive at this fearful place where at least we could sit down.

When we arrived, we were immediately surrounded by a mob of howling warriors. Jack and I were herded into the stockade and made to sit, still tied, with our backs to the rock, the very same rock face I had tried to climb so unsuccessfully and so often. As I glanced over at the roaring fire and the dancers, I was looking at the spot where my father's tent would be. Was he there now, worrying about my mysterious disappearance?

A few hours ago I had wished to be here. Now I wished to be almost anywhere else. The thought of what awaited us when the dance ended didn't bear thinking about.

"I fear, Al, that this is the end," Jack said quietly beside me. "I think these salvages do not wish to trade and our ending will shortly follow the one my father found so bravely this morn. It has been a brief friendship, but I am glad to have met you. I should have liked to have visited your home."

"And I would have liked to show it to you," I replied, shifting uncomfortably. "I'd also like to cut my hands loose. I think I've lost all the feeling in my arms."

"Wait!" Jack's exclamation was so loud I had to tell him to be quiet and not attract unwanted attention, but he spoke over my protests. "The arrowhead." I looked at his eager face in the firelight. "In my leather pouch. In the hut this morn when the salvages attacked I retrieved the head of the arrow that flew inside. I thought it might be of use. It is sharp. If you can fetch it from my bag, we might be able to cut the bonds."

In that moment I saw a glimpse of an escape. "Can you climb?" I asked.

"Passably well. I have scrambled over rocks in some strange corners of the world."

"Good. Could you climb this rock behind us?"

Jack tilted his head back and looked up. In the flickering firelight the face of the rock looked daunting—a patchwork of smooth, bright lumps and black shadows. I didn't think it was necessary to tell Jack I had tried to climb it and failed. It was the only way out.

"Perhaps," Jack said uncertainly.

"Good," I repeated with as much confidence as I could muster. "Then let's get our hands free."

Jack rolled onto his side with his pouch uppermost. By turning, I could just reach it. It was tied shut and I had trouble undoing the knot with my numbed fingers, but at last I succeeded.

The first thing I felt was the square shape of Henry Hudson's journal. It fitted snugly in the pouch and I had to slide my hand down its sides to search for the arrowhead. On one side was the gold angel; on the other was the arrowhead. The first I knew of it was as it sliced almost effortlessly through the skin of my forefinger. I had the unpleasant feeling of my skin being opened, but the arrow was so sharp there was hardly any pain. Working with less speed and more care, I grasped the broken fragment of shaft and extracted the piece of stone.

"Can you cut your bonds?" Jack asked, rolling back into a sitting position.

"I think so," I replied, turning the arrowhead in my hand. By grasping the broken fragment of shaft between my thumb and forefinger, I could hold it against the cords and move it, very slightly, up and down. It kept slipping on the blood from my finger, but the sharpness was now an advantage and I soon felt the bonds loosening.

I was so engrossed that I didn't see one of the dancers leave the group and approach us. Jack had to nudge me painfully in the ribs. I looked up to see the figure looming over us. It was the wounded warrior who had led us back here. His wound had been cleaned and his arm was strapped to his side. He was painted like the others and his head was shaved except for a topknot from which three huge eagle feathers hung. In his right hand he held the spear I had so carefully taken from the hut that morning.

Moving slowly, the man began his own dance in front of us. Mostly it consisted of stamping on the hard earth, but occasionally he would leap in the air. When he did so, he would wave the spear at us, often frighteningly close to our faces. It had to be some kind of test, so I determined to sit as still as possible. This seemed to work and the warrior spent more and more time taunting Jack, who flinched each time the spear was thrust at him.

At length the man tired of the game. I watched in horror as he took one last leap into the air and plunged the spear point into Jack's thigh. Jack's body arced forward in shock and pain. With a loud shriek the dancer withdrew the spear and flung it away before rejoining his companions beside the fire.

"Are you okay?" I asked urgently.

Jack's teeth were clenched and he was slumped forward. Gasping in pain, he leaned back and spoke. His voice was strained and his words were difficult to make out. "It hurts. I think it missed the bone and the bleeding is not too much. I do not think, though, that I will be able to climb your rock."

A faint smile crossed his face in the dim light. As he had been speaking, I had resumed working with the arrowhead. All at once the bonds fell loose and I could move my hands.

It took several minutes of painful movement to regain feeling in my hands and arms fully, and I had to be careful to keep them behind me in case any of the other dancers were watching. However, they all appeared absorbed in their activities around the fire. Leaning over, I cut Jack free.

"Thank you," he said, clenching and unclenching his fists. "Now you must be quick. The salvage may return."

"But what about—" I began. But Jack cut me off with his urgent whisper. "You must go! Climb the rock. When the feelings return to my hands, I shall try to find a hole on the fence and join you. But you must hurry."

I looked over at my friend. I saw the sense in what he was saying. Climbing the rock, difficult though it would be, was the best chance of escape. Even if Jack managed to find and crawl through a hole in the stockade, he wouldn't get very far with a spear hole in his thigh. If anyone was going to escape, it had to be me, and the way out was over the rock. I would have to desert Jack just as he had had to leave his father. The fact that there was no choice didn't make it any easier. Tears formed in my eyes.

All along I had known that my friendship with Jack was impossible and doomed, but I liked him. I enjoyed his company and listening to him tell of his life four centuries before my own. What had I told him in return? Suddenly it was very important for me to tell him at least some of the truth of my situation. It couldn't matter now.

"Jack," I began slowly, "I do come from a place called Ottawa, but it's not the way you think. My Ottawa is many centuries in the future. Somehow in the fog out in the bay I travelled back to your time."

Jack absorbed this information quietly, all the while staring intently into my face as I continued. "I can't explain it, but it's true. I know that you, your father, and the others weren't rescued. You all disappeared in the summer of 1611. What happened has remained one of the great mysteries of exploration. Your father became famous. The river you travelled up on the third expedition was named after him as was this great bay he discovered on this one."

Jack stared at me thoughtfully for a minute. "This explains much of your strangeness and the things you seem to know." He paused, then asked, "And the Strait of Anian to the north is truly blocked by ice?"

"Yes," I replied. "It won't be travelled for three hundred years and many men will die looking for it. It's not and never can be a commercial route from west to east."

I hesitated, not wanting to start explaining about air travel or even steamships. Jack surprised me with his next question. It wasn't about the wonders of the world of his future. "Why were you in the fog in your time?"

"Well," I began, thinking through my reasons as I spoke, "I was here, at this very rock, with my father digging in the remains of an old camp. We had found a coin, maybe the very angel you have in your pouch, and my father was trying to find more. No one believed him when he said that other Europeans were here before your father, so he had to find more evidence. The story your father told about the *Jonathan* proves that my father was right. But no one will believe that, either. The reason I was out in the fog was that I was feeling lonely. My father isn't easy to talk to. He's very wrapped up in his work and focused on proving his theories. I wanted to get away for a while."

Jack nodded understandingly. "I know what it is like to be lonely. My father, too, lived for one idea. Now you tell me the idea was wrong. At least his name is remembered. I was always closer to my father than my brothers. Very early I realized that I could not compete with his obsession. If I wanted to be with him, I would have to make it my obsession, as well. Thus I persuaded him to take me on his voyages. At least that way we were together. And that way I met you, my friend Al, and heard your strange tale. You have given me much to think on as I wait for what must come. But what of Juet, Greene, and the other mutineers? Did they perish in the Furious Overfall?"

"No," I replied, searching my memory. "Greene, I think was killed by Inuit, and Juet died of starvation, but some of the others made it back to England. Bylot did become quite famous as an explorer himself. We know what little we do from the journal kept by Abacuck Prickett."

"So Prickett's writings survived. I am glad. He was a good man and not one like Greene or Juet. You must go, Al, but I have one final question that your strange foreknowledge may be able to answer. What of my mother? Does the future speak of her?"

"A little," I said, recalling a small footnote I had read somewhere. "She struggled to get the government to search for your father, with little success, I'm afraid. Then she went to India where she became rich in, I think, the cloth trade. She returned to England and died a wealthy woman."

Jack smiled. "That at least is good. Thank you, Al. I do not understand this or you, but I am comforted by your tales. I shall not find my father again, but I hope that you find yours. "Now you must go," he continued more urgently, glancing back over at the fire. "The salvages are still busy with their dances and you must be gone before they think of us again."

Jack held out his hand and I took it. For a moment we sat looking into each other's face, friends across time. Then he released me. "Go!" he said. "And God bless you."

Tearfully I stood, turned, and began the climb. The ground level was lower by about a metre in Hudson's day, so the climb was longer, but the first couple of holds were easy, even in the poor light from the fire. The problem was the smooth overhang near the top. I felt almost naked in the flickering light and dreaded hearing a wild scream and the zing of arrows approaching.

I concentrated on the rock. What was it my dad always said? *The rock won't change. You have to adapt to it.*

The shadow beneath the overhang was pitch-black. This was where I always failed. The reach over the overhang was too long and my fingers couldn't get enough purchase to haul my body over. Maybe things would be different this time. Tentatively I reached up and over—smooth rock, polished by thousands of metres of ice grinding over it. I moved my hand from side to side. No handhold magically presented itself.

I began to sweat, even in the cool night air. I couldn't do it and the longer I stood here, the more chance there was that one of the dancers would look over and see me. That would be the end.

I strained to reach farther. It felt as if I were trying to stretch my body. Still nothing. The toe of my right shoe was on a tiny protuberance, and the fingers of my left hand were wedged into a small crack. Both my foot and hand were aching. I had to do something, or I would peel off the rock and crash to the ground below.

The rock won't change. You have to adapt to it.

That was it. I was thinking too linearly. At the camp with Dad the rock was an intellectual challenge. I deliberately took the straight route up because it was the most difficult. I wanted to defeat the worst the rock could throw at me. Now my goal was different. I wanted to survive.

Gingerly I retreated a step and scanned the face. To the right the overhang looked less daunting. Slowly I felt my way across the face. The footholds were more secure here where the moving ice had plucked out pieces of rock as it ground past. I reached up with my right hand.

Yes! There was a hold. I tested it. It appeared secure. Pushing up from my toehold, I took my weight on my arm and began hauling. My aching muscles and joints protested, but I got my left hand over and onto a grip. The overhang pushed uncomfortably into my belly and my arms felt as if they were on fire, but I was moving. I swung my leg up, got purchase, and pushed. Suddenly I was lying on top of the rock, gasping.

Rolling over, I looked back down. The camp was laid out before me, illuminated by the fire. Several rough huts and lean-tos were scattered within the enclosure. About twenty figures cavorted and danced close to the fire, still engrossed in their ritual. I looked down, but the overhang obscured a last view of Jack.

Slithering over the flat top of the rock, I scrambled down the much easier outward face and ran for the trees. It was a lot darker away from the fire and that, and my fearful desire to distance myself from the stockade, meant I didn't see the figure who threw out a hand that clamped firmly over my mouth while its companion locked itself around my body.

The warrior strained to make out the dark figure crossing the clearing from the *Iri-akhoiw* camp. The *okimah* and the war party had joined him and were crouched by his side.

"At least one to kill," the *okimah* hissed into his ear. But something was wrong. This figure was not one of the *Iri-akhoiw*. This was one of the captive boys.

"No," the warrior breathed back. "This is not *Iri-akhoiw*. This is one of the strangers. If he can escape, the spirits may yet have given us a way in to slay our enemies."

"We will capture him then," the *okimah* said.

The strange boy knew nothing of bushcraft, so the capture was easy. The warrior sat on him, hand over his mouth to silence him. The boy squinted up at him, his eyes wide with fear. The warrior placed his own finger to his lips in the sign for silence. Gradually the boy began to relax. The warrior slowly removed his hand, and the boy stayed silent.

"How did you escape?" the warrior asked.

The boy shook his head and said something the warrior could not understand. Rising, he pulled the boy to his feet. As the boy straightened, he became aware of the others in the war party and glanced around in fear at the dark shapes.

By repeatedly pointing to the boy, the stockade, and where they now were, the warrior managed to ask how the boy had escaped. It was slow. These strangers were certainly not intelligent, but at last the boy seemed to understand. He made signs to indicate the shape of the stockade with his clenched fist to mark the rock. Then he climbed the rock with the fingers of the other hand. So that was how he had done it—over the rock. Could the war party enter that way? The warrior doubted it. Even if they were undetected, the rock was only large enough to allow one or two over at a time and the *Iri-akhoiw* would be able to pick them off piecemeal. But perhaps one man could get in undetected and open the stockade gate.

With painful slowness the warrior repeatedly explained his plan in signs. It was frustrating because, any second, the *Iri-akhoiw* might notice the boy's disappearance and all surprise would be lost. Eventually, to the warrior's relief, the boy nodded. Good.

Hurriedly whispering instructions to the others, the warrior took the boy by the arm and led him back toward the stockade. It was very strange, the warrior thought, to be going into battle with one of the intruders. This was not what he had planned, but then the spirits often organized the world in unexpected ways. Reaching the foot of the rock, the pair began silently to climb. On the other side the dancing continued unabated.

TWELVE

Even in the darkness away from the fire, I realized almost instantly that the man who captured me wasn't the same as the ones in the stockade. He was wearing more clothes and had long, greasy hair hanging down on either side of his face. More important, he didn't try to kill me but merely held me down and kept me quiet. Then he tried to talk to me. I couldn't understand a word, but we did better with signs. I felt like an extra in a bad western TV show, but we made some progress. He wanted me to take him back into the stockade.

That was the last place I wanted to go but, apparently, this warrior and his companions wanted to attack the others, and that might be a way to rescue Jack. I had to go back.

As quietly as possible, I led my new companion over to the rock, which we both climbed easily. Lying on the top, I saw a view that hadn't changed in the few minutes of my freedom. That was a relief. It meant that my escape hadn't been discovered and that Jack was still safe below.

The warrior made a move to climb down into the stockade.

Worried what Jack might do if this stranger suddenly appeared beside him, I placed an arm on his shoulder. He turned to look at me and, by the firelight, I was able to make out his face for the first time. It was much less fearsome than the painted ones below, but it wasn't without ornament. Three black lines, which I guessed were tattoos, radiated from his lower lip to his chin. Three others ran horizontally across each cheek. Almost unbelievably, given our circumstances, he smiled at me. Instinctively I smiled back. Then I worked my way over to the side of the rock and began descending.

It was much easier going down than up, and I soon stood beside a surprised Jack. "What...?" he said before I motioned him to be quiet.

My companion arrived by my side. He stared hard at Jack for a moment, nodded once, and began working his way through the shadows along the stockade wall. I assumed he was going to attempt to open the gate and let his companions in. Silently I wished him luck. In the meantime I sat down beside Jack in case anyone glanced over.

We watched the warrior make his way along the wall, but could only see him because we knew he was there. His ability to use the shadows was uncanny, and he was only exposed for the briefest of moments as he flitted like a ghost from one to the other.

"I know him," Jack said at last.

"What? How?"

"He came to trade with my father last winter. I recognize the markings on his face. He was the only salvage we had contact with in the winter. He traded some skins for an axe, but he never returned. We tried to approach his village, but they fired the woods and fled. If they had helped us..."

"Then the mutiny might never have happened," I said, completing the bitter thought in my mind. But why should

First Nations people have helped Hudson and his men? They hadn't asked the intruders to come, and seventeenth-century sailors must have appeared incredibly weird to the Cree. It wasn't fair to blame them for Hudson's fate, and all the First Nations had paid dearly over the centuries whether they had helped the early European explorers or not.

My thoughts were interrupted by the growing awareness that the dancing had stopped. I looked up. Sure enough, there were no wildly dancing figures around the fire. Led by the wounded leader, they were all coming toward us.

Was this the end? Was I stupid to have come back? It was too late now to worry about that.

The wounded man led the way to us and stood over Jack. He carried a vicious-looking club in his good hand. Waving it about his head, he shouted at Jack, who cowered down as far as he could. This was going to be no slow torture; any minute the club would come crashing down and that would be the end of my friend. What could I do?

There was one hope. The warrior still assumed that our hands were bound. And there was the spear! After his last cruel visit, he had discarded it. Where? I looked about frantically. There! I lunged to my right. The warrior hesitated. That was his undoing. Grabbing the spear, I rolled over and threw it with all my might. It wasn't a well-aimed thrust, but it was enough. The spear scored a deep cut across the man's back. Howling in pain and rage, he turned toward me, club raised. From the other side of the fire madly screaming figures poured toward us. Arrows dropped a couple of our captors before they even realized what was going on. The rest turned to meet the threat, and the centre of the stockade dissolved into a chaotic mass of writhing bodies, lit eerily by the flickering firelight.

Jack and I rose and stood mesmerized. Who would win?

Would it make any difference in the long run?

It was fairly easy to tell the two sides apart, even in the uncertain light. Our captors' shaved heads and unclothed bodies were in sharp contrast to our rescuers' long hair, leggings, and shirts. The attackers appeared to have the advantage. As close as I could tell, there were approximately equal numbers on each side, but the shock of the surprise attack had unsettled the defenders and several of them were already lying on the ground. That gave the attackers an advantage in numbers, and they were using it to the full. Everywhere we looked it seemed that at least two of the attackers were swarming over a defender, stabbing, clubbing, and beating him down. They showed no mercy and only ceased when the body on the ground displayed no more sign of life. It was brutal, but I found it hard to feel pity. I had been scared too badly, and the attackers had probably suffered much in the past from these raiders.

The battle wasn't going to last long. I doubted if anyone could have kept up the violence of the attack or the desperation of the defence for long. There were only a few of the defenders still on their feet.

I was almost beginning to breath normally again when a figure detached itself from the throng. It was the wounded leader. Despite having only one usable arm, he must have fought ferociously to have survived this long. Now he was heading toward us, his body covered in blood and his eyes wild with hate. I glanced over, but the spear had landed too far away. The man was heading straight for me, bloody club raised. He was determined to exact revenge for the wound I had inflicted on him.

The only thing I could think of in the few seconds it took him to cover the distance was to try to jump aside at the last minute and then run as fast as I could. It wasn't a very good plan and, fortunately, I didn't have to put it into practice. The charging man was almost on me when he appeared to shudder. As if by magic, a long arrow appeared in his neck, the point on one side, the feathered shaft on the other. He probably died instantly, but his momentum carried him onward. I was so surprised that I completely forgot my plan and his body cannoned into me. I was thrown backward against the rock and my head hit with a blinding pain. Then I was on the ground feeling far away. The noise of the battle, the weight of the dead warrior on my legs, even the ground beneath me were receding rapidly. Everything was feeling less real, as if it were drifting away. Through the fog of my pain I heard a distant voice—Jack's.

"Al! Al! I think you are returning home. I will miss you. But I will always be by this rock to talk to you. Farewell."

It was a great victory. One that would be talked about proudly by the warrior's grandchildren's grandchildren. Every one of the hated *Iri-akhoiw* was dead. It would be many seasons before they dared venture this far into the warrior's territory again. The fools had been so intent on their dance that it had been easy for the warrior to sneak, unnoticed, around the stockade and open the gate.

The battle had been violent but short. Two of the warrior's people were dead and several others, including the *okimah*, were wounded, but that was a fair price. The dead would be mourned with honour and the wounded would recover in time, although the *okimah*'s arm was so badly smashed by a club that the warrior doubted it would ever be much use again.

The only thing that bothered the warrior was what had happened to the boy who had led him over the rock. The other had been found, wounded in the thigh and thin, but otherwise all right. He had been standing, dazed, at the foot of the rock. Of the other boy there was no sign. The warrior had searched, fearing he had been killed and that his body was lying in some dark corner, but he was not within the stockade. It was a mystery. To leave, the boy would either have had to pass through the battle or climb back over the rock. Both would be difficult, and the warrior could see no reason why the boy should want to run away. The warrior had made a special effort to do the boy no harm and to avoid frightening him. And the boy had smiled at him on the rock. It made no sense. Could it be that this stranger, who was different even from the hairy-faced one's band, was not human? Was he a trick of the spirits, sent to guide the warrior and his people to this great victory? He was like no spirit the warrior had ever seen before, but then who could possibly know all the ways and forms of the spirits?

The warrior shook his head in confusion. These were certainly strange times. The warrior looked over at the other boy standing amid the carnage. He looked frail and scared, and yet he was important. The warrior sensed that. The world was different now than it had been only a year ago before the strangers had come. In what way different and how this would all change in the future, the warrior had no way of knowing, but he was certain his world would never be the same again and that this boy was a part of the change. The *okimah* and the others would laugh at him if he tried to explain his feelings, but he was convinced of them nonetheless. The boy was important and something would have to be done with him. But what? At least there was some time.

The warrior let his gaze wander over the scene in the stockade. His companions were busy collecting their booty and dispatching any *Iri-akhoiw* who still showed a flicker of life. It would be a glorious homecoming, and the feasting and dancing would go on for days. Time enough then to think over the mysteries of the past weeks. Walking over to the boy, the warrior put a hand on his shoulder and said some reassuring words. Then, gently, he led the limping, frightened figure through the chaos of the stockade and into the darkness.

THIRTEEN

Al! Al! The voice kept echoing in my head. I recognized it, but I couldn't remember who it belonged to. My head hurt. In fact, my entire body ached. Painfully, slowly, I opened my eyes. I was lying at the foot of the rock where I had fallen. But much had changed. It was no longer night and the stockade, the battle, my attacker, and Jack had all vanished. Instead the sun shone high in the sky and my dad was standing over me, a look of concern on his face.

"Al, what's wrong? Are you all right? Where have you been?"

Shaking my head, as much at the barrage of questions as in an attempt to clear it, I struggled to sit up. Dad helped to prop me against the rock. Carefully I reached up and felt the back of my head. There was no blood, but there was a large, painful lump. Needing time to collect my confused thoughts, I took refuge in questions of my own. "What time is it? How long have I been out?"

"It's twelve o'clock," Dad replied, glancing at his watch. "I was just going to start making some lunch. I looked over and saw you lying here. You can't have been out long because I've been looking for you all over. What were you doing gallivanting off in the canoe and leaving me to pack up?" He paused. "But to be honest, I was getting worried, too. I was beginning to think something had happened. Obviously something did. What was it?"

I smiled involuntarily. It was so good to hear Dad's voice again, and I had been treated to more words than he often said in a whole day. And it was the same day I had left. I had only been gone a few hours. That made it easier.

Oddly the idea of telling the truth about my experiences never crossed my mind, perhaps because I had no answers to what had happened and, in any case, even I was a little unsure of the reality of it. Certainly it had seemed real and vivid when I was there, but a sense of the impossibility of it was growing rapidly in my mind now that I was back. I needed time to think things through, so a simple explanation would have to serve for now.

"I went out in the canoe before you woke up," I began slowly, thinking as I went. "I just wanted to be on my own for a while. I kind of hoped you would make breakfast while I was away, but I intended to come back in time to pack up. I guess I was preoccupied. Anyway, I drifted too far up the coast. This fog bank rolled in and got me all disoriented. I made it to the shore, but I put a rock through the canoe and had to walk back. I don't remember, but I must have slipped and hit my head coming around the rock."

The last bit sounded weak, but Dad didn't appear to notice. "Yeah," he said after a pause, pointing at my legs, which were covered with scratches and blossoming bruises, "you do look a bit beat-up. Do you feel okay?"

"Yes," I replied. "My head hurts, but it's just a bump and

the rest are just cuts and scratches. Some of that bush is hard to get through."

Dad nodded thoughtfully. "Well, look," he said eventually, "we're just about packed up, and the floatplane won't be here for an hour yet. You sit here and rest for a bit. I'll make us some tea."

"Sounds good," I said, relieved that I would have a bit of time with my thoughts. Dad moved back over to the camp stove and fired it up.

So what had really happened? I had gotten lost in some mysterious fog, travelled back in time four hundred years, met Henry Hudson, got mixed up in a local war, spent two days there, and got home in time for lunch. My instinct to say nothing about it had been right. That kind of explanation would land me in a psychiatrist's office before I could say Jack Hudson. But there had to be an explanation. Either it was some kind of complex dream or hallucination or...

Then I thought of something. Looking down at the index finger of my right hand, I saw an angry red line. It was one cut among many on my aching body, but I knew how I had received this one—on the arrowhead in the pouch that Jack Hudson wore.

I shuddered. Somehow, against everything that made any kind of sense, it had happened.

Watching Dad work, I let the warm sunlight soak into my body and thought back over everything. The excitement, the fear, the hunger—all had been real. And Jack. My friend. His last words came back to me: *I will always be by this rock to talk to you.* What had he meant? Instinctively I looked around, but there was no quaintly dressed boy standing beside me.

I shook my head again. No explanation fitted everything. The intellectual part of my mind rebelled at what I knew to be true. I had travelled in time. I was sure, but no one else would be. The coin proved nothing. I would have to keep this awesome secret for the rest of my days.

Then my stunned gaze fell on the disturbed ground where we had dug up the coin last season. A wild idea struck me with the force of a bullet. When I climbed the rock to escape the stockade, the ground had been almost a metre lower than it was now. That was where anything from Henry Hudson's time would be. So how could the coin have been on the surface? Then I remembered something Dad had told me about archaeology.

"One of the problems we have," he had said, "is that things move in the ground. Freezing and thawing every season, plant-root action, water-table changes, even the tiny movements of surface rocks, all have an effect. Hard objects, like arrowheads and musket balls, tend to migrate upward. In northern France, for example, unexploded shells and human bones from World War I, which were originally buried deep in the ground, are still showing up every spring on the surface of farmers' fields. Special bomb-disposal units drive the roads in ploughing season, picking up piles of these artifacts. Occasionally one will go off and injure or kill a farmer. Of course, the ploughing of the fields each year speeds up the process, but it does occur more slowly wherever there is any disturbance of the soil."

If that applied to an old shell or a human bone, then it could apply to a gold coin. Last season we'd only dug down thirty centimetres below the coin. We didn't go deep enough. Gingerly I got to my feet and shuffled over to where Dad was bent over the stove.

"Hi," he said, turning around. "Feeling better?"

"Yeah," I replied. "Have you packed all the trowels?"

"Yes, but they're just in that box over there. Why?"

"Oh, nothing," I said as casually as possible. "Just an idea."

"Okay, but don't go wandering off again. I'm making us some soup."

Quickly I picked out a trowel and returned to the rock. Dad watched me oddly as I began to dig, but he soon went back to his cooking. The ground was easy to dig through— mostly sand and small rocks, laced with a network of fine root hairs. It only took me a few minutes to get down as far as we had last year. Then the going got harder, but I still made good time. I wasn't using archaeological techniques, painstakingly checking each layer and sieving it, but then I knew where I was going.

After about ten minutes, I was down about as far as my arm could stretch. It wasn't a metre, but if I wanted to go deeper, I would have to dig a much larger hole. Then I saw it—a black line in the soil about five centimetres long. Carefully I lifted it out. It was a piece of leather strap. Jack's last words came flooding back to me. I knew what this strap was from.

I also knew I should call Dad over. This could be incredibly important, and I wasn't an archaeologist. My crude diggings could destroy valuable information. But this was mine. If what had happened was true, then this was a message to me. I had to find it.

As carefully as possible, I continued scraping the earth away. Other fragments of leather turned up. They were unrecognizable as anything definite, but I placed them carefully to one side. Then I found it. It was a rectangular package wrapped in heavy, oily, canvaslike material. It was brittle, but appeared in remarkable condition.

Not daring to breathe, I unwrapped the package. It was what I had thought—Henry Hudson's journal, which I had last come across as I searched for the arrowhead in Jack's leather pouch. My hands shook violently as I looked at the book and realized what it meant. Henry Hudson's story would be told at last.

With tears in my eyes I opened the book and peered at the ancient pages. There were words scrawled in a spidery hand by Henry Hudson himself. And what a story of horror and disaster they told. In here was Hudson's version of the mutiny and the answer to what had happened to the boat after it had been cast adrift. Also, somewhere in these pages was the story of the dying sailor from the *Jonathan*—the proof my father needed. The gaps I could fill in.

As I tried to come to terms with what I now knew had happened, I noticed something odd about the book. There was something stuffed inside the back cover. Carefully I pulled it out. It was a sheet of fine leather that unfolded to about the size of a regular page. On it were lines of tightly written script in a different hand from the journal. The spelling was odd, but it was quite readable:

On the Shorres of the Greate Sea,
Year of Our Lord, 1669

I am now welle into my seventy seconde Year and shalle not be likke to see another Wynter through. I have livved with the Salvages hereabouts since I was taken in by them as a Boy and now cannot be distynguished from them in either Speech or Dress. It has not been the Liffe I woode have chosen, but the Almighty saw otherwise. At the first I wyshed moste heartily for a Return to the Lande of my Birth, but I have comme to Acceptance of my Lot and even to the Enjoymente of it. Even to the Degree that this passt Year having the Opportunity to return to Englande with the Traders who are here wintering to trade for Beaver pelts I could not wyshe to do so. I even went among them unrecognised. I thought I would feel a Longing for that other Worlde but it was not so although I must admit to wyshing for one last Scent of "sweet smelling Beds of Lilies and roses, which Rosemary Banks and Lavender encloses."

For the most part, I found the Sailors of the *Nonsuch* coarse and even the Captain, Zachariah Gillam, to be an acquisitive Man. It was not their Fault, but rather that of their Worlde. I cannot return to that and must bid them Farewelle when they leave onne the Tydde the Morrow.

I will livve out the Days the Lord is pleased to give me in Peace in this Lande. I have seen many Wonderes, made Friends the Worth of any Gentleman, taken a Wyfe who has borne me three fine Sonnes and a Daughter, and have livved my Liffe to the fullest. My only Regret is that I was fated to lose my Dearest Friend Al. I do not know from whence he came or to where he vanished that Nighte so long ago, but I shall always remember him fondly.

I shall wrap this Document in my last Fragments of oiled Sailclothe, with the Journal of my Father that I have preserved all these Years, and bury them by the Rocke where last I saw my Friend. Perhaps...

But God will dispose of Thyngs as He will. I have seen a New Worlde but I fear the Arrival of this tiny Vessel from mye long forgotten Home presages a Sea Change which I thinke I would not wish to see. But whatever the Case, it is a Worlde my Grandchildren wille have to deal with. I wishe them much Fortune.

If you one Day by some Myracle read this Al, remember me fondly and use the Journal to enryche the Memory of my Father. I would rest now.

Farewelle again
Your Friend
Jack Hudson

I was overwhelmed. There was my name, penned in a document written three hundred and thirty-two years ago. Jack had survived. He had lived a long and, as far as I could tell, happy life with the Cree on the shores of James Bay. He had lived to see the *Nonsuch* arrive to begin the fur trade that would define the development of Canada and alter the First Nations' world forever.

"Al, soup's ready," Dad said, breaking into my thoughts.

Carefully I folded the letter from Jack and put it in my pocket. I felt a bit guilty concealing such a dramatic historical document, but then it was a letter to me and I would have a tough time explaining that. In any case, there was the journal and that would be enough to fuel a small industry among scholars for generations to come. And my dad would be at the centre of it.

I closed the journal and wrapped it back up in the sailcloth. Then I stood and turned toward the camp. On the breeze from the south I caught the faint buzz of our floatplane hurrying to take us back to the modern world and our futures. Oddly I felt no qualms. After what my friend Jack had been through and adapted to, I could do anything.

"Dad," I called, "I've found something. I think you should come and take a look."

The old warrior sat in the June sunshine, his back resting comfortably against the wide tree trunk. In front of him small groups of his people stood on the beach, looking out over the water. They were watching the large, ugly canoe as it struggled to fill its wings with wind. The warrior's mind drifted back many years into the past to another time when a winged canoe had visited his people. Then it had been different. The strangers who had come then had all died. All except *Dja-khu-tsan*, who was now almost as old as he was.

The warrior smiled ruefully as he remembered the enthusiasm he had had then for the strangers and their odd magic. He had been right. The strangers had returned, although it had taken them a long time. This time, largely due to his influence in the council, there had been much trading. The strangers had pulled their canoe completely onto the beach and built a large longhouse surrounded by a stockade of logs. They had fished and hunted in the fall and laid in supplies for the winter.

It had all looked so permanent that the warrior had wondered if they would ever leave. But leaving they were, with a canoe full of beaver pelts. The trading had been brisk all winter and his people had quickly realized that pelts that had been worn were more valuable than ones that were freshly killed. There would be much work this summer to replace the clothing that had been traded for the strangers' wonders.

Because of the trading the warrior's band was rich now. Everyone had needles, buttons, iron scrapers, and hatchets, and some even had the long sticks that made noise and killed game, or men, from a distance. Muskets, they were called. It was a far cry from the pitiful trading the warrior had done with *Dja-khu-tsan*'s people. And there would be more. It would not be as long until the strangers returned this time.

There would be more trading, of that the warrior was sure. And changes, too. He could not foresee what those changes would be, and he would not live long enough to see them, but changes there would certainly be. His people would use what they traded for and as a result want more. To get more they would have to hunt and trap more beaver to supply the needs of the strangers. Eventually they would spend all their time trapping and then they might forget the old ways of hunting and living off what the spirits of the land provided. What would happen then was lost in the mists of the future.

The only thing that was certain was that his people's way of life was going to change, and probably very quickly. That would be a shame, because it was a good way of life. So good, in fact, that *Dja-khu-tsan* had chosen to stay with them instead of returning to his home.

The old man smiled. He liked *Dja-khu-tsan*, who had become a good friend and a good *Kenistenoag* warrior. It had taken him a long time to learn the ways of the people, but now no one could tell he was not one of them. He had even visited the strangers' stockade, and they had not realized that *Dja-khu-tsan* was one of their own.

The warrior sighed. It was all so complicated now, not as it was when he had been a young man. Then life had been simple. He was glad he was not going to live to see the changes that were coming to his people. Reaching into a fold in his hide belt, the warrior pulled out the bright circle. It was the one the old *okimah* with the useless arm had given him. The warrior looked at the coin as it glinted in the sun. Several times he had thought of showing it to the strangers, but he had held back. There was another he knew. He had seen it in *Dja-khu-tsan*'s hand that night by the fire long ago, but had not seen it since. These strangers did not appear to have one, and if *Dja-khu-tsan* wished to make his known, then that was up to him. The warrior would keep his own and pass it on to the next *okimah*. And that would not be long.

Leaning his head against the friendly trunk of the tree, the warrior closed his eyes. No, it would not be long at all.

LOOKING FOR MORE ADVENTURES IN CANADA'S NORTH?

In this rousing young adult tale of the Arctic, John Wilson explores the vast territory of the 1845 Franklin Expedition, travelling aboard the ill-fated vessel HMS *Erebus* from London, England, en route to Canada's frozen and uncharted Far North. The adventures of David Young come to a modern-day Dave Young in Humboldt, Saskatchewan, in a series of dreams and strange coincidences. Is it possible they share more than a name?

ACROSS FROZEN SEAS BY JOHN WILSON

$8.95 CDN $5.95 US 128 PAGES

ISBN: 0-88878-381-7

TEACHER'S GUIDE ALSO AVAILABLE

In bookstores everywhere, or call 1-888-551-6655

BEACH HOLME PUBLISHING *WWW.BEACHHOLME.BC.CA*